CANADIAN RED

CANADIAN RED

R. W. Stone

**BLACK
STONE**
PUBLISHING

Printed in the United States of America

ISBN 978-1-5384-7468-6
Fiction / Westerns

1 3 5 7 9 10 8 6 4 2

CIP data for this book is available
from the Library of Congress

Blackstone Publishing
31 Mistletoe Rd.
Ashland, OR 97520

www.BlackstonePublishing.com

Dedicated to my wife, Rosi.

Twenty-seven years ago, a young veterinarian walked into my veterinary practice looking for a temporary job. She stayed on to become a permanent part of my life. Her job description of wife, mother, and professional associate truly doesn't do justice to her compassion, intelligence, good nature, and charm. The fact that she is beautiful and fun-loving doesn't hurt much either.

When in doubt, do right.

—Claude A. Swanson

CONTENTS

PROLOGUE

The Old West is filled with tales of roving outlaw gangs headed by now-infamous badmen. Almost everyone, Western aficionado or not, has heard countless stories of the notorious James Gang, the Daltons, the Younger brothers, the Clantons, Quantrill's Raiders, and Butch Cassidy and his infamous Hole-in-the-Wall gang.

The names of those remarkable individuals who enforced the law became just as well-known as those who broke the law. These men of frontier history include Wyatt Earp, Bat Masterson, Bill Tilghman, and Wild Bill Hickok.

However, when we think of the Old West only three professional law enforcement organizations immediately come to mind. The first would be the heroic Texas Rangers. The second group would be the now famous Pinkerton Detective Agency. The third organization, however, forged a legend all their own. They are recognized not only in their own country, but internationally as well. That unique band of men was made up of the courageous scarlet-coated constables of the Canadian North-West Mounted Police.

Think NWMP, and one special saying will surely come to mind: "A Mountie always gets his man."

PART I

CHAPTER ONE

It was a typical late-winter day in northern Canada. School had been canceled for the day, so the local boys and girls chose—for their fun day off—to go to the frozen pond that was just a mile or so outside of town.

The sun was shining such that had there been any adults around they would have thought the weather was a little warmer than normal for this time of year. They might have also noticed that the ice on the lake was thinner than it should be. In fact, instead of the pond being frozen solid, there were several spots where water was already seeping through to the surface. An adult would surely have been concerned about the ice's stability. But these kids were alone that day, and they were fearless and determined to enjoy their day in the great outdoors. Having toted their snowshoes, skates, and sleds, they spent the day playing, racing, and occasionally challenging each other to foolhardy deeds. The temperature was certainly the last thing on their minds.

"I'm telling you, it can't be done," Andy Peterson said, his words clearly meant as a challenge to his young friend, Lucas.

"I can, *too*, do it," Lucas replied stubbornly.

"You claim you can slide down that hill," Andy said, pointing to a nearby slope, "and when you come off the bottom curve, there, you say you can fly and slide all the way over to the other side of that pond, while still sitting on your sled." He traced the route in the air with his finger and then shook his head vigorously. "No way, it's much too far. It can't be done."

Lucas' twin brother Jamie looked up the hill, and then over to the far shore of the pond that marked the landing zone.

He shook his head slowly. "Looks kinda hard to me, too, Lucas."

Stubbornness ran deep in the Donovan family, and Lucas, in particular, was never one to stand down from a challenge.

The lad pulled his cap down tighter in defiance. "Yeah, well, we'll just see about that."

After pulling his sled up to the crest of a small hill overlooking the pond, Lucas began to map out his moves. His sled was his pride and joy, and he didn't want to damage it in this stunt. He always cared well for the sled, and, today, before they left home, he had waxed the runners with bear grease, so it would run fast and with less friction. He was as proud of it as any of his possessions. In truth, however, he had never actually tried to jump anything with it.

From his view high up, the pond suddenly looked a lot wider than he had pictured it in his mind. Nevertheless, even at ten years of age, Lucas didn't have an ounce of quit in him and he would never admit that he was afraid of anything, especially not in front of his twin brother and his friends.

The boy sat down on the sled and grabbed hold of the thick rope that steered its front end. He inched forward until the front half of the sled was hanging over the edge of the top of the hill. He took a deep breath, pulled his feet in tight, leaned forward, and ducked down as far as he could.

The sled practically flew down the hill, and, as he had calculated, when it hit the bottom where the hill sloped upward, the sled took flight. The crowd of children on the near bank of the pond threw their hands up and cheered as Lucas sailed out across the ice toward the far shore.

For a few moments it looked as though he might actually make it, but, as could be expected, gravity eventually took control, and the sled plummeted downward at a very sharp angle. Lucas gripped the rope tightly and leaned forward as much as he could, hoping he might gain a few extra feet, but it was useless. He crashed into the pond right where the ice was so thin it could not hold the weight of both sled and boy.

The next thing Lucas knew, he was plunging deep into the freezing water. Fortunately, he had managed to take as large a breath as he could seconds before breaking through the ice. The sled pulled him downward, but as soon as he was able, Lucas pushed back with his legs as hard as he could, propelling himself up toward the surface. He hoped to swim straight up and shoot right out of the hole he had crashed through, but the sled had entered at a steep angle. When Lucas finally reached the underside of the ice, he found it a solid sheet. The hole was nowhere to be found.

Cold and disoriented, the boy began to feel his way along the underside of the ice, trying to locate the lifesaving opening. For his age, Lucas was a strong swimmer, able to hold his breath a good length of time, but the cold, combined with his fear, sapped him of his energy and he soon began to panic.

Unable to cry out while underwater, he began praying, repeating over and over in his head: *Help me. Help me. Please don't let me die.* Holding his breath for as long as he could, he began to struggle, and just before he began to give up, he heard, or perhaps felt, a large splash in the water. Suddenly an arm reached out and grabbed the waist of his jacket and began pulling him over and then up through the elusive hole in the ice.

Once his head popped through the surface, Lucas inhaled the fresh air deep into his lungs, but that only made him cough uncontrollably. He began shivering uncontrollably as he realized that he had almost drowned, that he had been saved.

"Okay, boys, now! Pull with all you got," Jamie yelled.

He had a thick rope tied around Lucas' waist now and he was holding onto his waist tightly with his arm. The rope was stretched across to the pond's edge where the group of kids had stationed themselves, watching and waiting and worrying. They began pulling together, with all their might.

"Pull harder!" Jamie shouted, just as the two slowly came up and out of the hole and began to slide along the top of the ice. When Lucas began to shiver so hard that Jamie could hear his teeth chattering, he assured his brother that he would be fine.

"Not too fast!" a skinny redheaded kid shouted. "We don't want the ice around them to crack and suck them back in. It's hard enough pulling as it is, without having to drag them through the water."

One of the other lads, a towheaded boy named Jeff, dropped his grip on the rope and motioned for another one of the boys to follow him. "We need to get a fire started … as wet as they are, and as cold as it is, the two of them will freeze to death."

Children in the north woods learn survival skills at a very early age. Up there, you either learn how to deal with nature or you end up dying. Everyone, regardless of age, carried a fire starter or a pack of strike-on-anything matches.

As frightened as these boys were, it didn't take them long to gather kindling wood and get a good-sized fire going.

Once the brothers were finally back on dry land, the rest of the boys helped them over to the fire and out of their wet clothes. While they were drying off, several of their friends gave up their coats for added warmth and protection against the cold.

"Good thing I listened to Pa's advice," Jaime commented, shivering right down to his bones.

"How's that?" Lucas asked in what could only be described as a faint whisper.

"He told us never to go anywhere without a knife, a fire starter, a canteen, and a good long rope."

"How … how'd you find me down there?" Lucas asked.

"Well, I heard you calling me and just followed the sound," his twin answered nonchalantly. He seemed surprised.

Lucas was puzzled. "But I was holding my breath ... I was underwater. How could you hear me calling?"

Jamie shook his head and shrugged. "I don't know, I just did. You were repeating 'Help me, help me.' Weren't you?"

This pair just stared at each other and tried to comprehend what had just occurred.

"You saved my life, Jamie," Lucas said.

"Aw, go on with you. You'd have done the same for me, and you know it."

"Maybe, but that was a pretty big risk you took."

"Had to. Pa would have skinned my hide if I let anything happen to my younger brother," Jamie replied with a chuckle.

"Hey, you're only older than me by twenty minutes," Lucas reminded him.

"Well, a lot can happen in twenty minutes, squirt."

"Don't call me squirt. I'm the same size as you are, dammit."

The two fell silent as they stared into the crackling fire.

It was Lucas who spoke first. "Know this, Jamie, I owe you my life. From now on, wherever you go, I go. Whatever you might need, I'll be there to make sure you get it. Whatever, whenever, wherever."

Jamie smiled. "Same here, Brother."

"But just one thing, Jamie," Lucas said in a whisper.

"Yeah, what's that?" his twin asked.

"Please don't tell Pa about this. Ever!"

CHAPTER TWO

Several years later, when the twins were in their early teens, their father, Joshua, passed away unexpectedly. The elder Donovan's last will and testament stipulated that the ranch was to be left equally to his boys. The care of the twins and the operation of the ranch was left in the capable hands of Charlie Two Knives, their father's Cree Indian friend and helper on the ranch for years. For the twins, who loved and respected Charlie, he was the next best thing to having their father with them.

One Saturday morning in late autumn, when the three were heading out of the main house after finishing lunch, they saw a group of five men riding in.

It didn't take long for Charlie to assess this quintet, to know that they were up to no good. He unbuttoned his coat to allow faster access to the duo of belt knives he always carried, sheathed on opposite sides of his waist.

"Boys," the Cree said quietly, "I don't know these men, but I don't like their looks. You know what we have to do, so be ready."

"Hello, the house!" one of the men called out as they rode up.

The twins thought the man looked and sounded friendly enough, but just as they had practiced so many times in the past with Charlie, Jamie and Lucas walked away from each other and posted themselves on opposite ends of their front porch, right next to the wide wooden corner posts that supported its roof.

"How can we help you?" Charlie asked. His face was emotionless.

"Nice big spread you have here. The owner around?" The rider doing the talking looked to be around thirty-five and sported a long thick black mustache that hung down lower than his chin. "We'd like to have a word with him."

From the man's accent, Lucas thought he might be an American. He glanced at Jamie, who mouthed the word *Yank*. His brother nodded.

"You can speak with me, Charlie Two Knives of the Cree Nation. I run this ranch now."

"You? But you're a bloody Injun!" one of the other men exclaimed. He was short and thin, with blond hair, armed with a nickel-plated pistol stuck in the left side of the waist of his pants, butt-first, cross-draw style.

The first man turned to him and put his finger up. "Shut up, Joe. We agreed I'd do all the talkin'."

Joe stared at him a moment, then lowered his eyes and nodded angrily in agreement. "Fine. Do what you want."

"Look, Charlie, is it? My name's Hancock," the mustachioed man offered. "Sorry for my friend's rudeness. We're out scouting properties, looking to buy land in the area. We're interested in your ranch."

Charlie Two Knives was brief and to the point. "Not interested. It's not for sale."

"We can make you a very good offer. Big money. You know, much wampum. So, does that change things some?" Hancock asked.

Again, Charlie was abrupt. "No. It's not for sale at any price. There's nothing more to say on the matter." He raised his arm and pointed the way back.

Now a third man spoke up. He was wearing a long overcoat and had on a black stocking cap. "Look, you should really reconsider our offer, old man. There are other ways we can get your land, and none of them are very pleasant." His eyes moved from Lucas to Jamie. He paused for effect before adding: "And you have these two boys to think about."

"People who make threats are not welcome here. I'd suggest you leave now!" Charlie Two Knives, generally a calm soul, was clearly angered.

Hancock slumped a little in his saddle as if defeated. "Well, if there's no other way," he said, then cocked his head. "Go for it, Joe," he said quietly.

At those words, Joe pulled his coat back and went for his gun. He was fast, but not fast enough. As his right hand rose up, clenching that big pistol, a stag-handled, long-bladed knife flew effortlessly from Charlie's hand and embedded itself deep in the Yank's forearm. The gun dropped from his grip as he let out a scream of pain.

Startled by the man's sudden yell, two of the group's horses started to buck, and it took some effort for their riders to get them back under control. By the time they settled their horses and turned back around, they found themselves facing more than just one old Indian, handy with a knife.

From behind the porch beams, Jamie and Lucas had both pulled out hidden firearms. Jamie was armed with a large and menacing Sharps .50-caliber buffalo gun, and to his left his brother was brandishing a Greener side-by-side double-barreled shotgun. In the hands of the young twins the weapons appeared larger and more menacing than if in the hands of grown men.

"It's best for you to go before anybody else gets hurt," Charlie ordered, again pointing the way out.

"Hell, boss, we can still take 'em," the man with the overcoat urged.

A discharge from Jamie's Sharps rifle blew the hat off the man.

"Just because we're young, don't go thinking we don't know how to use these," Jamie stated, quickly reloading. "We been practicing since we were little. That Greener my brother's holding is a twelve gauge, and it can let go a powerful amount of hurt at this range."

It didn't take but a moment for the five intruders to make up their minds.

"Come on, boys, we're outta here," Hancock ordered.

As they turned to ride out, Lucas heard him say: "Joe, don't go pulling that damned knife out of your arm until we get a tourniquet on it, or you'll more than likely bleed to death."

Charlie Two Knives watched the road for a while. "They're gone."

"You think that'll be the end of it, or you think they'll be back?" Jamie asked.

"If they're smart, they won't," Charlie observed. "But we don't know these men. We must remain vigilant. But in the meantime, we have chores to do."

CHAPTER THREE

The next three weeks were relatively quiet and uneventful. Although the boys were never more than a step or two away from their weapons, there was no sign of trouble from Hancock and his men. Even so, since their visit, Charlie Two Knives, never one to be trusting of strangers, began taking afternoon naps and then staying awake late into the night in order to guard the ranch, in case the men returned.

It was on a cold Thursday of the fourth week that three men rode onto the ranch. The boys got ready to take up their positions on the porch as before, but Charlie held up his arm.

"It's all right. One of the men is from the trading post."

"Hey, Charlie Two Knives! It's me, Jeff Blake." The three men stopped their horses before approaching any closer. "Can we have a word with you?"

"Come in," the Cree replied. "Welcome."

"Hello, Jamie … Lucas," Blake said to the boys as he and his men neared the house. "Look I'm sorry to trouble you with this, Charlie, but there's been a problem, and we'd like you to come back to the post with us and discuss it."

"What problem?" Charlie asked, puzzled.

Jeff Blake pushed his hat back on his head, rubbed the side of his neck, and leaned forward in his saddle. "Well, it's like this ... Henry La Pierre has been killed."

The two boys gasped. Henry had been a friend to their father for years, so they had known him since they were little. He had always been a kind man, bringing hard candy for them whenever he visited.

"He will be missed. How was he killed?" Charlie asked.

"Well," Blake replied, "apparently he was ambushed a couple of miles from his place."

"La Pierre was good man, a good friend to Joshua," Charlie said. The Cree paused a moment, and then asked: "But what do you need with me?"

"Well, you know me Charlie, and I trust you. Still there's a lot of talk going around, and we'd just like to talk to everyone who knew him. You know, try to get things sorted out. As you say, Henry La Pierre was liked by most folk." Jeff Blake looked troubled. "So, can we get you to come in with us?"

The Cree thought for a good while. "I'll come, but not today. Tomorrow. We haven't been to the post in a while and we need some things. We'll come in with the wagon."

"We's supposed to fetch him back with us now," one of the men with Blake snapped rudely in Blake's direction.

Jamie and Lucas didn't like the man's tone at all.

"I've known Charlie Two Knives for years," Blake said to the man firmly, reining his horse around. "I've never known him to utter a single falsehood. If he says he'll come in tomorrow, that's good enough for me."

The man wasn't pleased, but he finally gave in. "Well, iffen you say so," he said, shrugging his shoulders.

The trader shifted around in his saddle and tipped his hat to the three on the porch. "Till then, Charlie. See you tomorrow, boys."

* * * * *

The next day was both cold and overcast. The twins had spent the better part of the night trying to convince Charlie not to go into town.

"I don't trust the way that one man with Blake reacted when you said you'd go tomorrow," Jamie argued. "I didn't recognize him."

"Remember the trouble we had with those other fellows," Lucas added.

The Cree's mind was made up, however. "I gave my word, boys. Without his word, a man is nothing."

At this point in their lives the twins knew better than to continue to argue with Charlie once he had made up his mind.

So that morning, they hitched up the wagon. As they were about to head out for town, the twins both reached for their guns.

"Leave those here," Charlie ordered. When the twins protested, Charlie remained firm. "We're not going in armed."

"You still have your knife," Lucas pointed out.

"I never go anywhere without my knife, a fire starter, and—"

"Rope and canteen?" Jamie said before the Cree could finish himself.

Charlie grinned. It was something he seldom did. "I was going to say brains, but you're right, you should always have a rope and canteen good, too."

The three started out toward the trading post, and while they knew they had done nothing wrong, they were still worried.

Traveling by wagon to the post took almost three hours. Since they hadn't been there for quite some time, the trio was surprised by all the changes that had occurred since their last visit.

A small town was now growing up all around Blake's trading post. There was a new hardware and general store, a blacksmith shop, and a small assay office—which for the moment was being run inside a large Sibley tent.

Charlie Two Knives drove their wagon up to the plank landing in front of the trading post and pulled to a stop. Lucas set the wagon's brake, and Jamie jumped down and went to the back of the wagon. He took out a rock that was tied with a rope and walked to the horses where he fastened the free end of the rope to the halter of the lead horse as a ground tie. Jamie had learned a long time ago that tying a team of rambunctious horses to a wooden hitching post could result in both a broken post and a loose team.

Blake appeared at his front door as the twins were brushing dust off their jackets. "Thanks for coming in, Charlie," Blake said, and nodded at Lucas and Jamie.

The Cree got down from the wagon seat, stiff from the three-hour ride, and began walking toward the trader. Suddenly there was a commotion down the street, and Charlie and the boys turned almost as one.

"There's the damned Injun what done it!" someone yelled.

Lucas recognized the man who shouted as the Yank called Joe, who had come to the ranch with Hancock.

"Let's get him, boys!" another yelled.

Despite his injured arm from Charlie's knife, Joe seemed to grow in confidence as men began coming out of the buildings and tents to find out what all the shouting was about. Joe walked slowly in the direction of the trading post.

"Wait a moment, men!" Blake cried out. "I told you we were going to hear Charlie out."

Jamie looked at Lucas with concern on his face, a growing queasiness in his belly.

"The hell we are!" shouted someone in the growing group of men. "It's Henry La Pierre we're talking about here. Never a finer man ... and now he's been murdered."

The old Cree kept his back toward the trading post as he watched the men, half of whom he did not recognize, gather in the road. A look of fear appeared on his weathered bronze face. "I wouldn't hurt Henry," he protested, glancing at Blake.

"What's going on, Blake?" Lucas shouted as he and his twin moved closer to Charlie in a protective stance.

"Henry was killed with a knife that looks like Charlie's," Blake answered nervously, backing toward the trading post door.

"They're going to kill him," Jamie said, "if you don't do something."

Five men broke away from the group, and were quickly catching up with Joe, who walked slowly and deliberately toward the post. He was only a few yards from the wagon when he stopped to wait for the others to catch up.

Then, like a hungry swarm of birds, the men descended upon Charlie. The twins tried to pry their friend loose from the grasp of men, but they were pushed aside and held back by the three others.

"Let's string him up!" came a voice from out on the street.

Jamie recognized the voice as coming from the man who had called himself Hancock.

"Over there! We can use that big oak." A man in a plaid coat said, pointing to a large tree with a thick low-hanging limb.

"I got all the rope we need!" another man cried out as he ran toward the red oak.

At the tree, one of the men grabbed one end of the rope and threw it over the large limb. Another jumped up and grabbed the dangling end of the rope and began fashioning a hangman's knot.

Held back by Joe holding a gun, Blake's protests went unheeded as Charlie was pulled toward the oak, his feet creating furrows in the cold ground as they dragged him. The twins were yelling and trying to break free, unable to understand how this could be happening, regretting that Charlie had not listened to them.

Charlie's hands were quickly bound behind his back as he tried ineffectually to break free of the men. But at his age he just didn't have the energy and the stamina to take on a bloodthirsty gang.

The twins were crying, worn down by the vicelike hold of their captors. They both dropped their heads as they watched a man slip the loop over Charlie's head and tighten it around his neck.

The men around the tree stood in anticipation, but several

looked hesitant, having been friends with Joshua Donovan. Suddenly an eerie silence fell over the group as several grabbed hold of the rope end, ready to hoist Charlie up. At the same time, the twins were released and shoved roughly against the trading post's wall. But there was no relief for them because there was nothing they could do to help their friend, since Charlie Two Knives had insisted they leave their guns at home.

Neither twin could understand how Hancock had gained so much influence and power in the town in such a short time.

"Blake," Lucas asked, "why is this happening? Who is this Hancock and how did he turn everyone against Charlie?"

There was no response from the trader, who looked as white as a ghost.

"Go ahead, pull him up!" Hancock ordered from under the oak.

All eyes were focused on the Cree when a shot rang out. The men turned as a lone man rode up, atop a large black stallion. The stranger held a Henry rifle and had it pointed in the direction of the men surrounding Charlie.

"Take that noose off that man right now and back away!" the man called out. His voice was deep and firm. Directing his aim at Hancock, he levered another round into his repeating rifle, as if to emphasize his words. He had on a buffalo-skin coat and wore a white pith helmet. The man's face was clean shaven across his sculpted square chin.

"There will be no hanging today, boys," the man announced with finality.

Someone in the group yelled back. "Yeah. Who says so? Who the bloody hell are you?"

"My name is Frank Davidson, and I order you to take that noose off right now."

Two of the men stepped out and removed the rope from around Charlie Two Knives' neck, and quickly backed away as Charlie collapsed to the ground.

Deliberately, the tall man replaced his rifle in the saddle scabbard and dismounted.

Hancock squared off and immediately challenged the stranger.

"I don't know why you want to get involved in something that clearly ain't none of your affair, but this man here murdered our friend Henry La Pierre, and we intend to see that justice is done."

"Is that so? Well, lynching someone without a fair trial isn't justice, so I'll take it from here if it's all the same to you."

"And what gives you the right to tell us what to do?" Joe shouted, moving over to the noose and grabbing it.

Never taking his eyes off Hancock, the stranger shook himself out of his buffalo-skin coat and tossed it over his saddle.

At the sight of the scarlet-red coat and the wide belt with a flapped pistol holster at its side, several of the men stepped back with an inhalation of breath.

"I am Constable Davidson, and my authority comes from the Canadian government. In the name of the Crown, I order you all to disperse." He walked straight toward Hancock and stopped only inches from him, facing him square on.

"He's one of them new North-West Mounted Policemen the government recently formed," Jeff Blake explained to the twins. "I sent for him."

"That so?" Hancock said, trying to appear in charge as he puffed up his chest. But his voice cracked a mite. "Well, that doesn't change the fact that this Injun here killed our friend."

The Mountie looked around at the other men. "What proof have you? Who says this man is the murderer?"

"We found this knife sticking out of Henry's back," Hancock said, producing the stag-handled knife. "Mister Blake, who runs the trading post here, he recognized it as belonging to the Cree." He handed the blade over to Davidson.

The Mountie turned the knife over in his hands. "Yes, it

does looks like a Cree could have made it. This yours?" he asked, holding out the knife so Charlie could see it clearly.

The Cree simply nodded.

The Mountie then placed the knife inside his own belt.

"See, he admits it," Hancock said, his voice brusque and dismissive.

As the Mountie stared down Hancock, the twins hurried over to Charlie and helped him get to his feet. They backed him up to a position behind the Mountie, feeling there was no one here, other than the Mountie, who they could trust, including Blake, a man they had been friendly with for years.

"That's a lie!" Lucas shouted in rebuttal to Hancock's statement.

But the Mountie ignored Lucas, and stepped back from Hancock, his gaze moving over the faces of the men under the oak.

"I wonder what motive he might have for killing a neighbor?" Davidson said. "And for that matter, what business is it of yours? You call Henry your friend, but you're an American, aren't you?"

"Yeah, we're from the States," the Yank replied confidently. "We came up here to invest in some land. No harm in that, is there?"

"No, none whatsoever," Davidson replied. "But again, what has all this to do with La Pierre's murder?"

"Well, it's easy enough to figure," Hancock said. "See, my friends and I got to know Henry pretty well. We told him about our plans and made him a very good offer on his land, and he agreed to it. We paid him, and Henry up and left his outfit with the cash money. Stands to reason this Injun must have found out about it. Must've hunted him down and killed him on the trail on his way outta here. It's always about the money, ain't it?"

Again, the Mountie nodded. "Oftentimes, yes, it is. Three things lead to murder in my experience ... money, jealousy, or anger."

"Right you are," Hancock agreed, gaining confidence at the thought of winning over the Mountie. He smiled in Joe's direction.

"Where's the money?" the Mountie asked.

"We figure the Injun must have hidden it," Hancock answered.

"So, it's really just your word that Henry was paid off, right?" the Mountie asked. "How much was it exactly?"

"Well, yes," Hancock paused, "but my four other friends were there, too, and they can swear witness."

"Of course. There is that," Davidson said, as he appeared to be thinking about what Hancock had said. "I suppose you have actual written documentation of the sale?" the constable asked.

All eyes turned to the Yank as his response wasn't so fast this time.

Finally, Hancock smiled. "Sure do. I got the bill of sale right here in my coat pocket."

The constable's hand drifted down to his holster, and he unfastened its leather flap.

"Nice and easy now," he warned.

"Sure thing," Hancock replied, slowing his movements. "You'll have no problem with me." He pulled an envelope out of his pocket and handed it over. "It's all right there in black and white. See for yourself."

Frank Davidson glanced at the paper, and then said: "Is Jeff Blake here?"

Blake stepped closer to the Mountie, saying: "Yes, I run the trading post. I'm the one who requested help here."

Without turning, Davidson handed the document over to the trader. "Hold onto this a moment for me, will you, Mister Blake?"

Blake nodded. "Of course, Constable. I'll be glad to."

Turning back to Hancock and the group of men, the Mountie continued his interrogation. "So, you're saying that after La Pierre took this money that you claim you paid him, he rode out. You believe that Henry must have come across Charlie Two Knives out on the trail, who then stabbed him in the back and stole all the money he was carrying? Do I have that right? Is that what happened?"

Hancock nodded, as did Joe.

"Makes sense, don't it, Constable? After all, Henry didn't have the money on him when they found his body. And he did have that Injun's knife sticking out of his back," he said, pointing at the Mountie's belt holding the Cree's knife.

The Mountie stood stock-still, his gaze driving into Joe.

Feeling there was finally an opening in which he could speak, Jamie said: "It's all a lie, Mister Davidson. Some weeks back, those Yanks tried to force us off our ranch, and when that man over there"—he pointed at Joe—"drew a pistol, Charlie threw his knife at him in self-defense. Last time we all saw that knife, it was sticking out of that man's right arm as he rode out."

"That's true, I was there, too," Lucas added.

"They's just trying to protect their friend is all. It's obvious he's guilty as hell!" Joe yelled out.

"Well, that's easy enough to prove," the Mountie said, his eyes shifting to catch a glimpse at Hancock before returning to Joe. "Roll up your sleeve."

Joe looked anxiously over at Hancock and back at the Mountie. "You ain't serious? You gonna take the word of these two kids over ours? Grown men?"

"Well, I couldn't help but notice that you do seem to be favoring your right arm a mite. Mind rolling up your sleeve?"

Jamie added: "When the knife hit his arm, he dropped his gun. It's back at the ranch."

"The hell with that," Joe cried, darting his eyes at the twins. "You can't prove the pistol is mine." He shifted his gaze to the Mountie and moved closer to him. "You want to see my arm ...," he started to say, then suddenly swung his left arm in a wide round-house punch that was aimed at the constable's head.

Frank Davidson lifted his right arm up to block the man's punch, then grabbed Joe's right arm and gave it a wrenching twist. The Mountie made it appear effortless, but it took its toll on Joe, who cried out in pain, cradling his arm as he dropped to his knees.

The officer quickly reached over Joe's back and tugged his shirt right out from behind his belt and pulled it up. Joe kept his arms locked, trying to fight Davidson from exposing his arm. However, the Mountie had no quit in him, and he yanked Joe's arm free and pulled the sleeve up, exposing his arm so the men who had backed him and Hancock could clearly see the bloody bandage covering the wound.

Several men moved forward and grabbed both of Joe's arms, pinning him down to the ground, Joe moaning as he tried to get away.

"Appears these boys were correct," Davidson said smugly. "Now all that remains is to see who was working with Joe here besides Hancock." The constable turned to face Hancock again. "So you still claim that you paid La Pierre and he gave you that bill of sale just before he rode out from his place that day?"

"Not a claim … fact. You already got the proof," he said, indicating the paper Jeff Blake was holding.

"Well, sir … that's real interesting. Mister Blake wasn't the only one concerned about the goings-on around here. You see, Henry La Pierre also notified the force about the trouble with land grabbers in this area. Did so by mail. Then Blake got in contact with us. So, when I heard La Pierre had been murdered, I rode over to his place and had myself a look around," the Mountie explained.

"There wasn't much out of the ordinary at his house … no signs of a struggle or anything of the sort. But while I was looking around inside, I stepped on a creaking board in the bedroom. When I pried that board up, I found a small metal box hidden underneath the floor boards."

By now the rest of the men in the crowd were listening intently to the constable's story.

"Inside the box was La Pierre's will. Seems that Henry left all his property, including his ranch and the mining operation that's on it, to his niece who is living back in Ottawa." The constable turned toward Hancock. "Now, why do you suppose he'd sell his land when he intended his niece to have it?"

Hancock's discomfort became obvious and he tugged nervously

on his mustache. "How the hell do I know? Maybe he didn't have a chance to change his will. Or … or maybe once he saw all that cash, he simply forgot about the will? Or maybe he just didn't care?"

The locals who had known Henry began to shake their heads as if disappointed in themselves for having been duped by the Yank, who was always talking big and throwing his money around.

The Mountie said: "Plausible."

Hancock seemed to relax slightly.

"Of course, since we now have your bill of sale, it's no problem whatsoever to compare the handwriting on it with the writing on Henry's last will and testament," Davidson pointed out. "And we have his letter to the force," he added as he handed La Pierre's will over to Blake. "Take a good look, Mister Blake." The Mountie crossed his arms as the owner of the trading post compared the two documents.

When Jeff Blake dropped his hand with the papers in it, Davidson said: "What do you say, Mister Blake, does the writing on the bill of sale match the writing on Henry's will?"

Before the trader could even reply, the other Americans who had ridden onto the Donovan ranch along with Hancock and Joe tried to make a run for it. At the same time, Hancock tried to bowl the Mountie over, but Davidson pivoted to his right and squatted down. The American was thrown over his back as the Mountie executed a classic hip throw.

The other three were grabbed by a number of the men—both locals and a handful of newcomers to the area, who had all become even more sheepish as the story unfolded—and were quickly hustled back in front of the constable and thrown down to the ground next to Joe. They were ordered to sit with their backs to each other.

As far as the Donovan twins could tell, the Mountie didn't appear to be ruffled even slightly.

With the Yanks in custody, Frank Davidson turned to face Jamie and Lucas. "You boys showed real courage and loyalty to your friend.

The force will need lads like you someday. In the meantime, would you two mind getting the handcuffs I carry in my saddlebags?"

The twins raced each other over to his horse.

"Mister Blake, may I use your trading post's back room as a temporary jail," Davidson asked.

"Yes, sir, Constable Davidson," Blake answered, keeping his eyes downcast, afraid to meet the eyes of Charlie Two Knives or the twins.

* * * * *

Throughout their teens, the Donovan twins would often talk about their first encounter with a tall heroic man in a bright scarlet Norfolk jacket who saved Charlie's life and helped the folks protect and keep their land, for no telling what lengths Hancock and his men would have gone to take over the area. So it wasn't surprising to anyone, especially Charlie Two Knives, that the two brothers joined the North-West Mounted Police once they reached their majority. Charlie's proudest day was when he saw the two young men in their NWMP uniforms.

PART II

CHAPTER FOUR

The long barrel of a Remington rolling-block rifle protruded through the thick brush sticking up through the snow. A tall, heavyset, bearded man sighted down the rifle's bore as he lay in wait. The man was positioned high up on a hill that overlooked a small but well-defined sled dog trail. It was seldom used anymore, but, even so, the man behind the gun was expecting company.

There was a word for what this rifleman was about to do—bushwhack. The sniper grinned to himself as he lipped the word, since he was in fact hiding in the bushes. While the man knew the word could describe a scythe, or the cutting of underbrush, or maneuvering a boat through water by pulling on bushes, he preferred its darker definitions which included a brigand, a guerrilla fighter, or an ambusher, which is what he was. And what this ambusher had in mind was murder, plain and simple.

He figured that the two men trailing him had to be following his tracks with the purpose of doing him harm. It mattered little to him that the law might rightfully be on their side. In fact, it mattered to him nothing at all. He had always felt that way. In fact, when a boy, he used to torture small animals whenever he got the chance, and he enjoyed the activity. He didn't give a damn about what other people might think about him or about what he did. All he cared for was his own personal pleasure and, as he grew older, his survival.

As evil as he might be, the bushwhacker was, nonetheless, an experienced backwoodsman. He knew how to track and stalk and how to prepare a blind. He had spent the last several years in the Canadian wilderness, wandering the back country, causing chaos and upheaval in the lives of others, taking lives without a second thought. He had gotten away with it because his crimes usually involved lone individuals who would not be missed, at least not for a very long time. He derived his greatest pleasure when he came across an isolated cabin with a small family that he could torture and kill.

Recently, the man-killer had shifted his hunting grounds from northern Alberta to the southern area of the province, which was more populated. And while he had found more targets, he also understood the presence of more people meant he was taking greater risks. He ignored those risks when he entered the small isolated trading post—home to a family of three—after observing them for several days. He had overwhelmed the proprietor, and then tied him up. He had been in no hurry, so while normally he would have shot the proprietor first, he decided he would let the trader watch while he had his way with his wife and his grown daughter. The very thought had heightened his feelings of arousal and pleasure.

Unfortunately for him, a pair of sled teams arrived before he had finished his work there. At the sound of the dogs, he had glanced out the window, and that had told him the two men on the sleds were both experienced woodsmen, and well-armed ones at that. He did not want to alert the two of his presence, so he dove out the rear window of the cabin and hurried off into the woods, to the sled he had hidden earlier. He had stolen it, along with its dog team—from a lone, unsuspecting, and now dead fur trapper—about a month back.

He wasn't surprised when the two men on their sleds had followed him from the trading post. He had known that there was always the chance of making enemies along the path he followed.

He did not know who this pair was, but what surprised him was how they continued to doggedly pursue him. Even with all his experience and skill at covering his tracks, this pair seemed able to follow his trail. Each time he thought he had eluded them, they would appear close on his heels, hounding him.

This man was not accustomed to being preyed upon by hunters—it was usually the other way around—and his frustration was mounting. He simply could not understand why these two cared about the trader and his family so much that they would not give up. Their persistence bothered him to such a degree that he had made up his mind to stop trying to get away from them, and instead to end their pursuit once and for all.

For a bushwhacker to be successful, he must be able to remain motionless and patient for long periods of time. This man never wearied of the wait. Nothing could interrupt or break his single-minded concentration and anticipation.

The plan he had laid out to end the two dog sledders pursuit began with laying down a false trail. He was confident that, unless this pair was capable of some sort of magic, there was no way to avoid his trap.

The man was sure the two sled dog teams would follow the path right below his current location. It was a narrow path that ran parallel to a steep gully. That would put them directly below his position, and so the outcome was certain no matter how long it took for them to appear.

The Remington rolling-block was only a single-shot rifle, but it was one of the most reliable buffalo guns on the frontier and could be reloaded very quickly. This particular one was a military model that had since been fitted with a new, long-range telescopic sight.

After several hours of waiting, he could hear the dogs in the distance. He watched as they appeared as specks, far out yet, but the gap was getting smaller and smaller. As they came closer, the features of the man in the first sled came into better view in the scope of his rifle. But the man in the second sled had a scarf wrapped around his face that made it impossible to make him out. The shooter did not recognize the man in the lead, not that it would have made any difference. Now all that was left for him to do was decide which man to shoot first, the one in the lead or the one in the back.

There were pros and cons to either choice, but he finally decided on the lead musher. It stood to reason the one in front was likely the more aggressive of the two, and, besides, once the driver in front was dead, his sled would jam up the team following behind, thus allowing for a clear shot at the second man.

The Remington was already cocked before the two sleds passed near his hidden position, and another shell lay ready on the ground next to his rifle for a quick reload. The bushwhacker quickly calculated the distance and the downhill trajectory, and he aimed. When the lead team's driver glanced up again, the shooter saw the man's face clearly magnified through his rifle's telescopic sight. He adjusted his aim slightly and fired.

Coldly and without a trace of remorse, he had sent a bullet right into the chest of the lead driver, who, upon impact, was thrown off to the left of his sled and then rolled down into the gully below. The shooter quickly reloaded and sighted his rifle on the second man. As the second dog team slowed, he watched its driver jump off his sled, rifle in hand.

He ran toward the edge of the gully where his partner had fallen. As he passed the front of his team, he reached down in a quick and natural movement, unhitching the enormous sled dog that was in the lead. He paused at the edge of the gully and looked down. He then turned and raised his own rifle as he searched the ridge for some sign of the shooter.

From that particular angle, the man's raised rifle blocked the larger and therefore easier chest target of the shooter, so, taking aim from hiding and without further hesitation, the bushwhacker fired off a head shot at his second target. His heart began to beat in excitement when his prey was hit and fell backward. His body, just like that of the other man, rolled down the steep slope and into the ravine below.

The sniper didn't even bother to check on the condition of the two men, so certain was he of his own skill. One man shot dead center in the chest and the second downed by a head shot at this range. He shook his head. They were both dead. Of that he was sure.

CHAPTER FIVE

The bright white snowflakes swirled around in ever increasing intensity. At the bottom of the deep gorge two bodies lay, belly down, on a mound of snow. The blood from their wounds had already begun to freeze.

The arms of the two men appeared to be intertwined. After a while, one of the men began to stir. He felt a presence and gradually began to recognize the sound of a beast panting. He felt its cold wet nose sniffing all around his face. The animal's nose blew warm air into his face and his wet tongue repeatedly licked and slobbered on him. He heard whimpering. Moving his body required an immense effort and could only be done in small increments, but eventually he managed to sit up.

The wounded man's forehead had a longitudinal gash up under the hairline, but the winter cold had already caused the blood to clot. Head wounds often look worse than they actually are, and this was fortunately the case for this man. After wiping his eyes with his coat sleeve and using handfuls of the surrounding snow to jolt himself wide awake, the man found himself looking into the eyes of his big red-and-white Alaskan malamute.

Even though the man's head hurt, he still managed a small smile. "Good boy, Red. Good dog, but get back now."

The big dog took a few steps backward as instructed, but, for some unknown reason, he didn't stop his whimpering. Then the malamute started to paw the ground around him.

The man struggled to his feet as the wind blew his unbuttoned buffalo-skin coat open to reveal the scarlet-red tunic of a North-West Mounted Policeman.

"Jamie … Jamie, get up," Lucas said, reaching down to shake his brother who lay crumpled on the snow-laden earth. The limp form did not stir or respond in any way.

Lucas had a terrible sinking feeling. "God, no! Jamie, no!" he cried out, dropping to his knees, understanding dawning on him. After taking in a few deep breaths, he gently rolled Jamie's body over and stared into his own face, the eyes open but unseeing. The full realization of what had happened and what it meant was almost too overwhelming to take in.

When the Mountie began yelling at the top of his lungs, the malamute, Red, and the nearby sled dogs all began to howl along with him in an eerie symphony of pain and despair. All the while the man hugged his brother's body, rocking back and forth, crying alone in the white wilderness at the bottom of the gorge. The tears began to freeze on his cheeks.

When he felt physically able, Lucas Donovan lifted his brother, a fellow Mountie, up over his shoulder. But it proved to be too much weight and he quickly became light-headed and dizzy. He set Jamie down, picked up his Enfield rifle, and called out to Red. "I need your help, boy," he told the malamute. As he grabbed one of Jamie's arms and started dragging him, Red understood, and bit down on Jamie's coat and started pulling him up the hill along with Lucas.

Lucas was a large man—most of the men in his family had

been—but in spite of his size and strength, the trek up the frozen side of the gorge seemed nearly impossible. Blood loss, the cold, and grief played a role in his weakened state, and several times Lucas almost gave up.

If Joshua Donovan had taught his two sons anything, however, it was that family meant everything—and that no son of his should ever consider giving up once he was committed to a righteous course of action. Lucas might die trying, but he would not leave his brother lying at the bottom of a lousy ditch out here, alone in the middle of the Canadian wilderness.

After an exhaustive struggle, Lucas and Red finally reached the top of the ravine. There he found the two dog sleds right where they had been forced to stop earlier in the day. The two teams of dogs were resting in the snow, but they perked up when Lucas appeared over the edge of the gully. Lucas placed Jamie's body in the basket of his own sled, covered it in a thick brown tarp, and then tied it down securely.

He tied the two sleds together and hitched his and Jamie's dog team together, his team in the lead. He located a canteen and drank his fill. Starting with his big red-and-white malamute, Lucas then examined all the dogs. They seemed fine, even though his brother's dogs seemed agitated by Jamie's absence. Since the sled teams had been well fed earlier in the day, the Mountie only had to water them before beginning the long trek back to the fort.

It had been Lucas' long-standing habit to release his lead dog, Red, whenever he left the sled. Red was powerfully built, and in Donovan's expert opinion there was no better lead dog in the Canadian Rockies than his big malamute.

The Donovan twins had begun training sled dogs when they were in their teens, building doghouses and a dog run they could use in the summer months. Lucas had raised this particular dog from a pup as his personal pet. Since then, they had never been separated, the force allowing him to use Red as part of his sled team. In all his years, Lucas had never seen a dog as devoted or as strong-willed as Red. Lucas often wondered if maybe it had something to do with his coloring. Around these parts most malamutes, like their Siberian husky counterparts, had coats that were primarily black and white. His dog, however, had the less common reddish-brown-and-white colored coat.

If there was one thing for sure, it was that wherever Lucas went, Red went. Donovan had learned years back that if he left Red alone, tethered to the sled or a rope, even if he was leaving just for a few minutes, the dog would literally tear apart his tether, harness, and leathers, and then run after him. After losing too much equipment and unable to train it out of him, Lucas automatically unhitched the big dog whenever he left the sled. Today it turned out to be a God-sent gift, as it was Red who had helped bring Lucas back to consciousness—as well as getting Jamie up the hill.

The wounded Mountie found a strip of cloth from his pack, which he wrapped around his head wound—about which he had been unaware until he was back at the sleds—and then painfully readjusted the big fur cap he was wearing. He winced as he pulled the cap down over the bandaged gash. Lucas adjusted his gloves, checked the buttons on his coat, and tied a scarf around his face, as the wind was picking up. He then took Red over to his position at the front of the lead team and attached his harness.

Before heading out, Donovan made sure all the tack was properly in place on the dogs. A harness that is fitted correctly will lie flat on a sled dog's back, go between the dog's front legs and stretch across the last rib. The very tip of the harness needed to end at the base of the dog's tail. To do otherwise can cause things to tangle, or, worse yet, create bad sores along a dog's body that can easily become infected.

Donovan moved to his place at the back of his own team. After taking a look back at the second sled that was carrying his twin brother's body, he said softly: "We're going home Jamie." Lucas then called out to both teams.

"Let's go, boys. Mush!" He used the bastardized term used by the English Canadians, taken from the original French trappers' term *marche*.

The dogs pulled at their harnesses, and though the dogs started off slowly, not used to a double burden, they were soon moving at a fast pace. For Lucas Donovan it would be a harsh two-week trip back to Fort Macleod. It would be two long weeks, filled with loneliness, memories, and the cold hard realization that he would never again experience that unique and special bond that he had shared with his twin brother.

CHAPTER SIX

Some hours later, Lucas made camp in a stand of aspen trees that he picked because the snow was not deep there, and because he knew various uses of aspens he'd been taught by Charlie Two Knives.

Charlie was a *Nehiyawak* or Cree Indian. Lucas' father, Joshua, had been out hunting, and he had found the Cree Indian he called Charlie lying near a fallen tree, injured. Joshua Donovan had nursed him back to health. A bond of friendship blossomed during Charlie's recovery, and the Cree decided to stay on and help Joshua with his expanding ranch. The boys had never gotten the story straight, but apparently the name Two Knives was either a translation from his native tongue or was a nickname bestowed on him by their father because of the Cree's amazing abilities with knives, both as a tool and as a weapon.

When Donovan's wife died as a result of complications from childbirth, Charlie Two Knives was there to help raise the twins, a gift Joshua felt he had been given and for which he could never repay.

As the Donovan twins grew up, Charlie Two Knives educated them, as best as he could, both to appreciate the Canadian wilds as well as how to survive in them.

"Nature can be a blessing or a curse," he would remind them

over and over. "She's a changeable creature, dangersome but giving. Respect her power and you will have a much better chance at survival."

Heeding both Charlie's counsel as well as their father's advice whenever he gave it, the Donovan boys grew up to become strong and capable woodsmen.

As Lucas set up camp, knowing he was low on matches, he removed a small hatchet from his sled and walked over to a large aspen tree where he proceeded to chop into a big knot in the bark that makes an excellent fire starter—something he had learned from Charlie. When the knot was chopped out, Lucas placed it on the ground and loosened its interior. Removing a fire stone from his pocket, Lucas struck the edge of the hand ax on the stone, and in no time at all the sparks ignited the inside of the tree knot's bole. Once he had the fire going, he could heat food for the dogs from the supply the Donovan brothers always carried on their sleds.

That done, Lucas took a few minutes out to sit down, exhausted. His head was throbbing with pain now, and he was nauseated, having a hard time thinking. As he lay back by the fire, he thought back of the information Charlie had given them on healing properties of things you could find in the wild.

He remembered that, once, when the twins were about eight years old, their father came stumbling in through the door all scratched up and bloody. He had been out trapping and had stumbled across a cougar on the prowl.

"She jumped me from a tree branch. Never heard or saw her till it was too late," Joshua Donovan had explained.

"How'd you get away, Pa?" Jamie and Lucas wondered in astonishment.

"When she knocked me down, I fell amongst some rocks. While she was pawing me to hell, I managed to pick one up, and I bashed it over her head. That ended that, thank God Almighty. My legs and arms didn't hurt much at first, but they sure bled a lot. I can barely use them now, and they hurt something fierce."

Charlie Two Knives had tended to the scratches and gashes. He started by washing the wounds. Then he told the boys: "Go outside and find buds from last year's aspen growth. The buds are medicinal, good for pain. Look for the darkest part of the twigs. The inner tree bark is good for pain, too, when scraped off."

Head throbbing, Lucas now began the work of gathering the things he would need to brew the natural medicine for the pain in his head. He knew that what he needed was all around him. He started water boiling for the tea. He then collected several of the aspen buds and ground them together with the scrapings from the inner lining of the bark to add to the brew. While he was waiting for the tea to heat, he also chewed on the twigs. Although relief wasn't immediate, once he drank the concoction, the pain eventually subsided, and the warmth made him much more comfortable.

Next Lucas gathered together the aspen's outer bark and scraped off the light powder that forms on its outside. He applied the soothing powder to his face as it had become chapped from the snow and cold.

When the fire began to dwindle, Lucas cleared away a patch of snow near the sleds and sleeping dogs and got the hand shovel from Jamie's sled. In the cleared area, he dug a trench, which he filled with the hot ashes and glowing embers from the fire. He covered the coals over loosely with the dirt. By placing his sleeping blanket right over the coals and dirt, Lucas knew the radiant heat from below would protect him from the cold all though the night. The last thing he did before stretching out was to check on Jamie in the sled. He gently patted the tarp that held his brother and told him good night.

Red kept watch for a while, but he finally walked over and curled up alongside his master. Before allowing himself to drift off and forget about the day, Donovan checked his rifle and pistol one last time. It turned out to be a restless night for Lucas, despite his exhaustion. The young Mountie tossed and turned while nightmarish images of his brother's death played out over and over in his sleep.

In the morning, when Lucas first awakened, there was an instant when all seemed well with the world. It wasn't until he turned to check on his brother, as was his habit, that he remembered what had happened the day before, and it hit him like a punch in the stomach. He wasn't sure how he could go on alone without his brother. Slowly, that sadness turned to something else, something dark and terrible. It turned to anger, hate, and a burning desire for revenge.

Standing over his twin's cold body, Lucas swore a personal oath to track down his brother's killer and to make him pay the ultimate price for what he had done.

Once he had the teams lined up and the equipment stored or ready, he went to his place on the sled, yelling out to Red and the rest of the team: "Home, boys! Mush now, mush!"

CHAPTER SEVEN

It took twelve days before Donovan pulled the two sleds in tandem into the town of Macleod, located in the southwest corner of the province of Alberta. The fort that was located there had originally been named in honor of Colonel James Macleod and was now home to the Canadian North-West Mounted Police force.

Lucas pulled his team to a stop in front of the building that housed the headquarters for his unit. He knew that inside was Major Hank Milton, the current commandant of the NWMP here in the district.

Milton was a trim and fit man in his early fifties, known for his steady disposition. He was the type of leader who would not ask anything of his men that he was not willing to do himself. The men of the NWMP recognized that characteristic and respected him for it.

Before entering the office and reporting to Major Milton, Donovan glanced around the grounds of the fort. It felt comforting to be back, and his eyes scanned the barracks on the fort's east side, across from the buildings that housed the rest of the men working inside the fort. Then he took in the guardhouses, the hospital, and stores to the south. Behind him, to the north, were the stables and the blacksmith's shed.

The fort had been relocated here about three years earlier, and at the time Lucas had thought it a good idea. It stood to reason that, sooner or later, railroads would link Macleod with the rest of Canada, and eventually even down into the States.

After being out on the trail for so long, Lucas found it reassuring that everything, here at least, seemed in order and unchanged. He proceeded to unhook his big malamute from the sled, after pulling off his thick gloves—which he secured in the wide leather belt he wore. Next Donovan removed his fur hat, revealing the scabbed-over wound on his forehead, and wiped the inside of the its brim before settling it back on his head. He was now ready to talk with Major Milton.

Donovan entered the headquarters office. Inside, he stopped a couple of steps in from the doorway, stood at attention, and saluted sharply.

Sitting behind the desk, Major Milton removed his briar pipe from his mouth with his left hand and returned the salute with his right. "Welcome back, my boy. Tell me, how'd it go?" Because the force had been hearing about people going missing and a number of murders in the north, the twin Mounties had been sent out on patrol to learn as much as they could about the reports.

"Have a bit of a rough time, eh, Corporal?" he asked, pointing with the stem of his pipe toward Lucas' forehead when he took off his hat.

"What I have to report, sir, well … I'm afraid it isn't very good," Lucas replied with hesitancy.

Major Milton sat up straight. "Say, where's your brother Jamie? Walking in again?" It had long been Jamie's habit to get off his sled after a long patrol and walk the final mile into the fort. He said it helped get the cramps out of his legs and clear his mind before reporting in.

With a pained expression, Corporal Donovan shook his head. "Outside, sir. He's dead, sir. His body's outside … in his sled."

"No! Not your brother, lad," the major gasped, not embarrassed to show his distress at the information. "I'm truly sorry, son," he said. "He was a fine Mountie. You two were a solid team ..." His words trailed off when he realized what he was saying would only make Lucas feel worse. "Sit down. I'll have men take care of Jamie and tend to the dogs." He got up, went to the door, and called out the order to Sullivan and Smythe.

His anger festered as he thought about the loss to the force with the death of Jamie Donovan. As he sat back down behind his desk, he asked for details. "Tell me what happened, Corporal."

"We were ambushed out there, sir," Lucas began as he slumped down into the chair. "We were after this fellow, name of Emerson, Jack Emerson. Jamie and I were certain that he's the man who has been doing all this killing and terrorizing up in the north. And we were getting close to him, but he tricked us, set up a false trail. He must have doubled back to lay in wait for us. When we got close to his blind, he shot Jamie. Got him right in the chest. Got me, too, but I was luckier than Jamie."

Major Milton nodded, cleared his throat. He considered things for a moment before saying: "A service will be held tomorrow. I want you to check in with the doctor, and, after he clears you, take the rest of the day off to recover from your ordeal. We can talk more tomorrow."

Lucas started to protest, but the major held up his hand as he rose from the desk and headed for the door. "I'll make sure everything is readied. Whether you feel it is necessary or not, I want the doctor to have a look-see. That is an order. Understood, Corporal Donovan? Oh, and draw yourself an extra ration of rum."

Following the commandant through the door, Lucas nodded his head. "Understood, sir, and I thank you."

The major gestured to some of the onlookers. "Lucas, I assure you, the men will take good care of your brother. I will get a full report from you after we have taken care of this very sad business."

The corporal saluted, turned sharply, and then stepped outside.

"Come on, boy," Lucas said to Red. "Nothing we can do here. Jamie's in good hands now."

Patting the dog on the back, Corporal Lucas Donovan walked slowly toward his barracks with the massive red and white malamute trotting faithfully alongside him.

CHAPTER EIGHT

"For as much as it has pleased the Almighty to take out of this world the soul of our friend and comrade, Jamie Randall Donovan, we now commit his body to the earth. Ashes to ashes, dust to dust, waiting for that day when the Lord himself shall descend from heaven …"

At that point in the funeral service Lucas' thoughts began to wander. Almost everyone from the fort had come to the ceremony conducted by Major Milton and the local pastor. He wished that Charlie Two Knives was still alive to be here, but he had died of pneumonia last winter.

Lucas felt conflicted. On one hand, it was gratifying that everyone at the fort thought so highly of his twin brother. That almost down to a man, they had wanted to pay their respects. But on the other hand, Lucas could not help feeling an overwhelming sense of impatience, knowing the man who had killed Jamie was still on the loose. Lucas couldn't help but feel that standing around reciting platitudes and feeling sad was counterproductive to what he had in mind: revenge.

After the ceremony, the major motioned for Lucas to join him in his office. Once inside, the two men pulled up chairs in front of the desk. The room was spacious, but relatively spartan in design and decor, considering the number of years Milton had been in the force. There was a small picture of the Queen hanging on the far wall and a small certificate signifying Milton's promotion next to it. The near wall held a large framed map of the province. On the major's desk was a picture of his wife and daughter, an ashtray, a pipe holder, an inkwell, along with a messy pile of miscellaneous papers. Now it also held the family Bible used in the memorial, which the major had set there when they entered the room.

"I want you to know, Lucas, that you have our sincerest condolences," Major Milton began in a kindly tone. "I also want you to understand that every officer in the province will devote all they have to catching this Emerson fellow, dastardly coward that he is. I assure you, we shall all make a point of seeing to it that this bastard is brought to justice," the major added hotly, for the more thought he gave to this Emerson, the angrier he became. "Nobody kills a Mountie and gets away with it."

Corporal Donovan nodded, but his eye kept being drawn to the map on the wall. "Excuse me for a minute, Major," he said as he got up and walked over to the map. He studied it for a while before speaking. "You are going to let me handle going after this man, aren't you, sir?" he asked somewhat anxiously, fearing the answer he might get.

Major Milton shifted uncomfortably in his chair, and then cleared his throat. He slowly lit his pipe, sending up a cloud of smoke that he watched swirl in the sunlight coming through the window. Fort Macleod's commanding officer seemed lost in thought and didn't respond, didn't even seem to be aware of Lucas for a number of minutes.

Eventually, he tapped his pipe nervously in his left hand, and said: "You know as well as I do what the official policy is in these situations. Allowing relatives of the deceased into an official investigation is risky for all concerned. I know how you must feel … vengeful and grief-stricken. But these feelings could adversely influence your judgment in the field. That is precisely why the force's policy is to reassign those in your position to other duties or place you on administrative leave."

"But with all due respect, sir, I think I know this Jack Emerson better than any other constable in the force at this point. Jamie and I got close to him. *I* need to be out there, going after him. We trailed him for weeks. You know I have the best chance of catching him. It may be the official policy, sir, but don't they leave you with any discretion in these matters?" Lucas had to pause so he could calm down, unclench his fists, appear detached from his feelings. "This is just plain wrong, and, begging your pardon, sir, I think you know it."

The major thought about what Lucas said for a moment, then he shook his head, saying: "I still have to report back to my superiors, and, besides, I'm not sure I do disagree with that particular policy. You weren't just fellow constables, you were brothers. You need to clear your mind and heal from your loss, gain some perspective. Might do you good to leave the manhunt to others."

Having his hands tied in this manner was the last thing Lucas Donovan had expected. There were so many thoughts whirling through his head that, for a moment, he actually considered resigning from the force. Deep down he knew he would have to be the one to settle the score with Jack Emerson. He also knew arguing with Milton was pointless at this juncture, but, as he waited silently to be dismissed, a way around the policy occurred to him.

Nodding slowly as if he finally agreed with his commanding officer, Corporal Donovan studied the major as he walked back to the chair. "You mentioned something about an administrative leave?"

Milton's pipe having gone out, he tamped down the tobacco in the bowl before bringing a match to it. He puffed a couple of times and again appeared to be considering Lucas' words. Milton was, if anything, a very deliberate man. When the major finally looked up, Lucas was once again staring at the map.

"Yes, that's right," Major Milton replied slowly.

"Well, sir, in that case, I'd like to take mine now."

"Corporal Donovan," the major said sternly, "I knew your father and I had great respect for him. I do believe I have a fair appreciation of who and what it means to be a Donovan. Believe me when I say that you aren't fooling me one bit. You have no intention of going on leave, Corporal. The first chance you get, you will be back on this Emerson's trail, and we both know it."

Looking again at the wall map, Donovan replied: "What if I give you my word that I will take my leave across the border, in the States, and not involve myself in any of the investigation here in the province? Would that convince you, sir?"

The major considered Donovan's proposal for a moment, then nodded. "Might make a difference ..." He paused. "Once you are on leave and have sworn an oath to me that you won't involve yourself in any of the force's activity here, then I will have no further say in the matter. As far as the NWMP policy is concerned, during a leave you are free to do as you wish. It would leave me in the clear should questions arise ..."

"Yes, sir," Lucas assured Milton, and paused as he weighed this alternative. Then: "Well, sir, I believe that is just what I'll do. A trip across the border might help put things in perspective. Maybe it's about time I took a vacation. You won't have to worry about any breach of conduct here in Canada."

"Very well," the major replied, looking relieved. "Now tell me everything you can about Emerson, eh?"

"Well, Jamie and I stumbled across a backwoods cabin during a snowstorm up north," Lucas began. "We found a man inside, half dead from a couple knife wounds. They looked bad, but, maybe because it was so cold, the bleeding had slowed ... or brought his heartbeat down ... I don't know. Anyway, he was breathing. We got a fire going in the cabin's stove and we nursed the man, a fellow named Joseph Grant, and finally he was able to talk. Seems Grant had spent some time with this Jack Emerson," the corporal explained. "And, Emerson did some talking about places he had been, especially when he drank. He bragged about some things he done. Grant became scared for his own safety. Then one day, the two got into an argument over something trivial, and Emerson stabbed Grant. He said he felt like he was looking into to the eyes of the devil when he did it, too.

"Well, sir, we spent a number of days with Grant, but despite our best efforts, he finally succumbed to his wound. Infection maybe. We buried him there near his cabin—which wasn't easy in that frozen ground—and then over the next few weeks we trailed south, looking for any sign of Emerson. Along the way we found one fellow who had been robbed, and we heard reports from others of men missing, assumed dead. The description given by the man who was robbed matched Grant's. A powerful, solid-built man, not that tall, rough-looking.

"Seems Emerson thinks pretty highly of himself and doesn't believe he's ever in the wrong. Grant thinks he enjoys hurting people. But Emerson's arrogance might bring about his downfall eventually. He just assumed that Grant was dead, or would die from the wounds, so he simply up and left him there in the cabin. A more careful criminal would have checked to make sure his victim was dead, but not Emerson. Same thing when he shot Jamie and me. I didn't see any tracks in the snow indicating that he had come down and checked on us to see if we were dead.

"Anyway, after a week of trying to pick up his trail after leaving Grant's cabin, we'd just about given up. We started south, and we came upon this small trading outpost, run by a family named Stanton. Very isolated. Emerson was there when we arrived, though we didn't know it. He was inside ... using the womenfolk, mother and grown daughter ... um ... let's just say ... immorally and viciously. Horace Stanton, husband and father, was tied up. Stanton said when Emerson heard us, the man jumped out of the cabin window. Apparently, we had startled him before he could do whatever he was going to do.

"At any rate, after doing what we could to help the Stanton family, we headed out after the man, both convinced it was Emerson, based on the description the Stantons gave us. Jamie took the lead once we were that close to him, because, as you know, he's one of the best trackers on the force."

"So that was close to the time you two were shot, eh?" Major Milton said, moving the story along.

Corporal Donovan nodded. "Yes. But instead of us catching him, he caught us. He set up a false trail that led us right into his hands. We both fell for it. As I said, he's a skilled woodsman. I don't know how he had the time to set the trap for us."

The major sat back, mulling over what Donovan had said while puffing on his briar pipe. "Now, lad, show me there on the map where these encounters happened."

The two walked over to the map, and Lucas pointed to an area. "Grant's cabin was here"—Lucas moved his finger down the map—"and the Stanton outpost was here, farther south."

Major Milton stared at the wall map. He traced a path with his pipe stem. "And you were ambushed …?"

"Here," Lucas said, pointing to a spot below the outpost. "He's working his way south, sir. Or at least he was at the time we were tracking him."

"And you think he's still headed south?" Major Milton asked.

"Before he died, Grant told us that Jack Emerson has ties in the States—his family has land at a place called Willard Creek in northern Idaho. Can't find it on our maps. We were on to him, sir, and he knows it. I think the pressure was getting to him, which is why he ambushed us. He knows we'll be tightening the noose, so to speak, especially if he figured out we're Mounties. And like you've said over and over to us, sir, nobody kills a Mountie in Canada and lives to tell it. Emerson has to know that. Even if he didn't recognize us as constables at the time, he'll hear about it soon if he stays around. You know how fast word of this kind of thing spreads."

"If he's as arrogant as you say, he might think it clever to double back and return north," the major opined.

"Yes, sir, he could," the corporal agreed, "but we'll have a ring around the whole province. And as the noose tightens, that will force him south again. If my fellow Mounties find him anywhere in Alberta, I'll be a very happy man, but if my theory is correct—"

"That's why you want to go down to the States," the major interrupted.

"Off the record … yes, sir," Donovan answered.

"I don't like it. Don't like the idea of you going down there after him," the major added. "The force can't afford to lose another good man. And you will have no one to back you up—as well as no jurisdiction."

"I will be careful," Donovan replied.

Major Milton sat quietly, before he spoke. "How are you planning to travel?"

Lucas considered the question for a moment before replying. "I think I should take the train south, then buy a horse in the States. The train will get me there faster. I'd like to get there ahead of him, but I don't know if that's possible. Emerson may be a lunatic and a cold-blooded killer, but he'll be watching his back trail, and I have no intention of walking into another ambush. There's an old Scottish adage: 'He that deceives me once, shame fall him; if he deceives me twice, shame fall me.'"

Major Milton nodded in agreement. "Well worth remembering that one. Sounds to me like you thought this out rather thoroughly, Corporal Donovan," the major said, "but please remember you'll have no jurisdiction once you're across the border. You will have to rely on local law enforcement to bring him in, and if he isn't wanted in the States, they may not want to help. But keep in mind, you are working on a theory."

"Well, sir, if I'm wrong, then either he'll be brought to justice up here by a fellow constable, or he'll disappear forever. It's a calculated risk either way you look at it," Lucas stated. "As for relying on the local law once I cross the border, it may become a matter of self-defense for me."

Major Milton looked over at the corporal very sternly. "Be very careful with that one, Lucas. Very careful. Like you said, this man is a lunatic, but he's a smart one." The major paused as if considering another point. "Remember, I haven't any idea of your plan. But I'm giving you my blessing privately. Before I forget, there's one more thing. Your brother Jamie left a will. I understand Mister Hendricks over at the bank is the executor of his estate. Before you leave, I suggest you stop over there and check in with him."

"Certainly, Major," the corporal said, feeling satisfied. "Is that all?"

"That's it, Lucas. And Godspeed to you."

The corporal put on his white pith helmet, which he had exchanged for the fur cap he had worn when out on patrol, and saluted the major."

"I'll be back, sir. You can count on that."

The major returned his salute. "Make sure of it, Corporal. Dismissed."

CHAPTER NINE

"You have my deepest condolences, Lucas," Hendricks, the banker, said as he took Donovan's hand in his and patted it. "Here, my boy, please take a seat. I want you to know I always felt your brother was a fine man and an asset to our community. His loss is deeply felt by all of us who knew him."

The Mountie took a seat in front of the banker's large desk. "Yes, sir, thank you. I appreciate that," Lucas replied as he glanced slowly around the small office. "I'm here for two reasons, sir. First off, Major Milton said something about Jamie having a will. I wasn't aware he had made one."

Mr. Hendricks nodded. He was a heavyset man in his fifties with a balding head and a double chin. He was wearing new spectacles since the last time Donovan had seen him. Apparently, they didn't fit well since they kept sliding off the bridge of his long, beak-like nose, and he kept having to push them back up and adjust them every few minutes.

"Yes, Lucas my boy, Jamie did. Came to me almost a year ago. Said he wanted to put his affairs in order in case anything ever happened. He explained to me that he knew the chances you constables take, and should anything ever go wrong, he didn't want anyone taking anything that might rightfully belong to the Donovan family. At least not his part of it."

"I knew Jamie tended to be a more concerned about things like that than I ever was, but I never suspected he worried about it quite so much," Lucas commented, still surprised that Jamie had never mentioned the will.

"Guess he didn't want to burden you with such an unpleasant subject," Hendricks said, shrugging uncomfortably, which made his glasses slide down again. "At any rate, this morning, I pulled out his documents and reread them." Hendricks raised an eyebrow.

"Yes, sir. Thank you, sir," Lucas answered

The banker smiled. "You don't have to *sir* me, son, I work for a living."

Donovan chuckled. It had become a common saying in the force among the noncommissioned officers, and it had always made the twins laugh.

"Shall we begin then? Jamie left you his half of that big ranch your father gave you two boys. You are now the sole owner. He left you his savings in the bank here, which amounts to a little over four hundred pounds, and also that Sharps fifty-caliber rifle of his. Said it was the one thing of his you always admired … and he wanted you to have it."

"Our father," Lucas interjected, "originally won it in a poker game that lasted all night. He pulled a royal flush against a full house. He wasn't dealing at the time, so the other fellow couldn't accuse him of cheating. It's a real beauty. Not the sort of firearm I would choose for this line of work, but, for a hunter, there is nothing better for big game."

Hendricks looked back down at the paper on his desk. "Let's see now, what else? Oh, yes, you also get your father's pocket watch and a stag-handled knife carved by Charlie Two Knives."

Lucas thought back to the day Jamie got the knife. It was his—their—birthday. Jamie got the knife and Lucas received a beautiful bearskin coat. Charlie had spent months making their gifts. The coat was warm and had served him well over the years, but, at the time he had been given it, Lucas thought he'd rather have a knife like his brother received. Reflecting back on the current turn of events, Lucas regretted his petty jealousy.

Mr. Hendricks shuffled the papers on his desk, and then explained that the remainder of Jamie's possessions—uniform, harness and tack, the sled and his own dog team—he bequeathed to the North-West Mounted Police to use as they see fit. "So, Lucas, do you have any questions or concerns about your brother's will?"

Lucas shook his head and smiled. "No, Mister Hendricks. I reckon Jamie knew what he wanted and what he was doing. It's fine with me."

The banker sat back. "You mentioned that there were two things you wanted to discuss. What is the other?"

"I'd like to take out two hundred in gold coins, and then leave the rest in an account that I can have access to while I'm on leave," Lucas explained.

"Certainly, Lucas. That will not be a problem for us. Two hundred in gold coin, you say?" Hendricks asked.

Lucas had already estimated his travel expenses. "Yes, sir, and I want to be able draw on the rest, if and when I need it."

"Shouldn't be a problem. Going on a trip, are you?"

"Yes."

Hendricks considered the request for a moment. "You're going down into the States after the man who killed Jamie, aren't you?"

The corporal considered his answer carefully, wondering how the banker had learned about his trip. "Now, Mister Hendricks, let's just say, I'm taking a leave of absence. I need a break for a time to think about my future. After what happened to Jamie ... I need a little time for myself."

"I understand, Lucas," the banker said unconvincingly.

"And now with Jamie's money added to mine," Lucas plunged on, "I'm sure the money in my account will be more than sufficient for anything that comes up. However, in the event that I might need funds beyond what I have in cash, I can put up my part of the ranch as collateral … actually the whole ranch now … can't I? I'll sign any papers you need. Anything unexpected happens to me, the bank will own it free and clear. Four hundred acres of prime land with river irrigation and a large ranch house, stable, corrals, and dog houses and runs already built. By doing this, I will have a guaranteed fund should I need it. And the bank will have little if any risk."

The banker nodded. "No, under those circumstances we sure wouldn't, but truthfully, lad, what are you really going to do?"

"That, sir, with all due respect, will remain my concern, not yours," Lucas replied with deadly earnest.

"Maybe not my problem, but it will be a worry of mine, I assure you."

"So that settles it," Lucas said somewhat anxiously.

The banker reluctantly nodded in agreement. "Swing by in the morning to sign papers and pick up the gold."

"Thank you. I appreciate it."

"Lucas," Hendricks said as the corporal was about to leave.

"Yes, sir?"

"Get the bastard for me, too, would you?"

Lucas smiled back at the banker. "Don't know what you're talking about. Like I said, I'm just going to take some time off."

Hendricks nodded back. "Of course. But there is one more thing."

"What's that?" the Mountie asked.

"Do me a favor and take Jamie's Sharps rifle with you on your … vacation."

CHAPTER TEN

Lucas Donovan started packing early the next day. He rolled up his scarlet tunic and gray pants, tying them up with his uniform's leather belt. For this trip he would wear civilian clothes—flannel shirt, denim pants—under his buffalo-skin overcoat. Instead of the white pith helmet, Lucas chose to wear his Stetson. It was a pinched-top, flat-brimmed campaign hat, which was quickly gaining favor among the constables in the force. It was far more practical, and, more importantly, it was far more comfortable.

Before leaving his barracks, Donovan belted on his holster with the .455-caliber Webley Mk I revolver that he always carried. Earlier that morning, Lucas had picked up his money from the bank and, after signing the papers that would turn over the ranch to the bank should something happen, Mr. Hendricks presented him with a money belt.

"I've used this from time to time," the banker told him. "It comes in handy. Take a few coins out for daily use and put them in your pocket. Carry the rest in this belt, under your clothes. Less chance of getting robbed that way."

Lucas examined the money belt. With his gold coins inside, it was admittedly a little heavy, but once around his waist and adjusted, the belt seemed more comfortable than he would have expected.

He had considered his options for traveling south and finally decided to take a dog sled cross-country to the nearest train station to the south. There he would leave the sled and dogs with the stationmaster. He made arrangements for someone from the fort to retrieve the dogs. Red would travel with him to the States. Leaving him behind was simply out of the question. They had been through far too much for too long for Lucas to travel anywhere without his constant four-legged companion.

After packing his sled, Lucas said his goodbyes, took one last look around the fort, and headed out the gate. The team was well rested, and the dogs stepped out energetically. At the pace they struck, Lucas figured on reaching the train station in about two-to-three days' time, barring any problems.

Donovan always enjoyed running his sled with a good team, and this was one of the best he'd ever trained. The team was made up primarily of malamutes and huskies, but there were two wolf-hybrid crossbreeds in the pack. As usual, big Red was at his place in the lead position. They were making good time.

* * * * *

It was about three in the afternoon when Lucas crested a high mountainous peak that overlooked the railway tracks below. Even though the trail here was rougher and more dangerous, he had chosen to take this cross-country back route in order to save time.

Off in the distance, Lucas could see smoke rising from a train engine, but he wasn't particularly concerned about arriving on time. A train had to follow wherever the railroad's winding tracks led, whereas, traveling as he was, Lucas could take any number of routes, including several short cuts he knew.

As he looked out, taking in the panoramic view, a rumbling noise began and grew louder to his left across the valley. Startled, Lucas looked over, and to his horror he saw an avalanche come crashing down on the tracks around a curve still some distance from the train, but in its path. The Mountie knew instinctively that at the speed the train was traveling, its engineer would never be able to stop the train in time. He wouldn't even see the huge mound of snow because of its location on the far side of a curve in the tracks.

Lucas' heart began to pound. He knew this was a passenger train, and if it hit the massive snowbank with any kind of speed, there would be a derailment and certainly a loss of lives. The problem for him was how to signal the train from his location way up on the crest of the hill. Shouting or even shooting wouldn't be heard over the sound of the train engine, especially at this distance, and even if the engineer did hear the gunfire, he wouldn't know that it was a warning.

Donovan looked down into the valley. The slope he was on was practically vertical, so it would be impossible to run a dog team straight down it. There was simply no way dogs could run straight downhill with all that weight behind them. The sled would pick up too much speed, overtake them, and because they would not be able to free themselves, they would be dragged and tossed about, and more than likely end up being killed. The Mountie shook his head as he scanned the land, trying to come up with a way to stop the train. Then it came to him—just what had to be done, even though it was a risky—and Lucas quickly unhitched the team and pushed the sled to the brink.

It would take far too much time to travel all the way around the hill and down into the valley with the dogs. What he had in mind would probably be suicidal, but he knew it was his best chance at stopping the train. There were lives at stake, so he had to do something, and he couldn't come up with any other ideas. He unharnessed the excited dogs, and then stowed the equipment on the sled to give it weight. He gestured for Red to follow the trail with the other dogs and hoped he would know what to do once he saw the sled take off.

Climbing aboard the sled, Lucas took in deep breaths, then shook his head as he looked down the slope, recalling the foolish stunt he had tried as a young boy which had nearly cost him his life. Lord knows, he'd come close to death several times over the years. In lieu of a prayer, he said aloud: "I may be joining you soon, Brother, so if you can put in a good word for me with the boss, I'd surely appreciate it."

Someone once said that courage is being afraid, but saddling up anyway, and now Lucas Donovan was about to saddle up.

The young Mountie knew that Red would find a safe way down into the valley and he would bring the other sled dogs with him. What he didn't know was whether or not he would still be alive when they finally found their way down to him.

Lucas let out a yell and pushed off. The dogs started barking.

The momentum of the sled increased so quickly it took Donovan's breath away. It felt to him as though he were flying straight down the slope. Donovan had to force himself to keep his eyes open, since he needed to watch out for any obstacles along the way—even if most were buried under the snow. At this angle and speed, even a small rock or branch would send him flying into the hereafter.

Flattening himself out, Lucas used his body to rock the sled, making small adjustments in direction as he plummeted downward. Twice the sled went airborne, but luckily both times it landed upright on its rails as it continued on its downhill trajectory.

"Lordy mercy, Mother Mary, and all the saints in heaven!" Lucas yelled as the sled flew downward. Slowly the land began to level out, but the sled maintained its speed like an unstoppable projectile, shooting across the valley floor. When it finally hit the railway tracks, the sled flipped end over end and across to the other side of the embankment. Lucas was thrown more than ten feet into a nearby snowdrift.

Miraculously, the Mountie wasn't hurt. Dazed for a minute, he forced himself upright, cleared the snow from his face, and tried to steady himself. His knees were still trembling, and he was trying to catch his breath and gather his thoughts as he swallowed down an urge to vomit. It was then that the sound of the train whistle brought him back to his mission.

Lucas stumbled over to the sled, threw off his bag, and dragged the sled onto the tracks. He grabbed the Sharps rifle and a few other items from the pack and tossed them out of the way. Then he opened his traveling medical pouch, removed a small bottle of alcohol and proceeded to wet a patch of the sled. Lucas couldn't locate his fire starter as he dug through the pack, but fortunately he had a small matchbox in his front pocket. Still shaking from the downhill experience, Lucas tried to light a match. The first one wouldn't light; the second was blown out by the wind. All the while the train was rapidly approaching.

"Come on, Lord, a little help right about now would be nice," he said in exasperation, just as the last match in the box took hold and started the alcohol ablaze.

As the train approached, Lucas stood up and started waving his arms back and forth as the flames from the burning sled grew taller. Soon smoke began to billow around him, but as the train engine kept bearing down on him, all he could do was yell at the top of his lungs: "Stop, damn you! Stop!"

Almost as if on cue, the engineer pulled back on the air brakes, and the wheels reversed themselves, bringing the train to a halt less than a hundred yards from Donovan's position on the tracks. The young Mountie sighed with relief before collapsing to his knees.

CHAPTER ELEVEN

The engineers and the railroad personnel appeared slowly, jumping down from the train cars to investigate the crazy man on the tracks. Donovan was helped up by the conductor, and, after his heart slowed down, he explained in a hoarse voice why he had stopped them. The men surrounding him, at first angry and suspicious, were now relieved to learn how they had been spared from a sure disaster. They clapped him on the back and couldn't stop thanking him. As he stood talking with the head conductor, an older man named Herman, a few crew members headed back to the train to retrieve shovels.

Then Lucas heard the barking of Red and the rest of the sled dogs. He could barely call out Red's name, but soon the team came bounding down the hill and across the level ground. Red almost bowled over his master in his joy at having found him.

"That's a damned big dog you got there, son," Herman remarked, as he smiled and ruffled Red's head.

Lucas had to push Red back to stop him from licking his face. "You're right about that," he replied, "but there isn't a better sled team leader in the province." Looking over his shoulder, he shook his head and shrugged. "I sure hope you have a lot of shovels on the train. It's a big mound of snow."

"Shovels we got. Now the question is, how long is it going to take to clear the tracks and get out of here?" Herman asked, scratching his head.

The passengers who had emerged began to form a circle around the strange snow-covered man who had saved them and the train. "How about it folks?" Lucas asked. He held up his badge and waved it around for all to see. "I'm with the NWMP. What do you say … can we count on your help to dig out and clean off these tracks, so we can get this train moving again? It may take a while, even with everyone pitching in."

A young woman pushed through the crowd and looked deeply into the eyes of the Mountie. Lucas couldn't help but feel a tightening in his chest. She had the most beautiful face he had ever seen. Her eyes seemed to sparkle and were an unusual shade of violet.

"Before anything gets started here, I think something needs to be said," she announced, still staring at him as if she were sizing up a prize bull for sale.

Oh, great, Lucas thought to himself. *This is where I get blamed for delaying the train.*

"I think we need to thank this man for saving our lives," she said, smiling. The passengers who had gathered outside broke into applause and several cheered. Donovan blushed, which clearly did not go unnoticed by the young lady with the violet eyes. "And please, for heaven's sake, don't tell us you were just doing your job," she added.

The Mountie laughed, trying hard not to fixate on her eyes. He forced himself to look away, adjusting his hat as he turned to the train crew. "How about we start distributing those shovels?"

Passengers who could not shovel, for whatever reason, insisted on staying outside. Several men returned to the train and located a couple of axes. Within no time, several small trees were felled and cut up, and fires were started near the train and over at the avalanche area. Blankets were brought to help fend off the cold by anyone who needed them. The able men grabbed up the picks and shovels they could find and began the long and arduous job of clearing passage for the train.

They attacked the mountain of snow in shifts. Passengers and crew worked the rest of the afternoon, through the night, and most of the next morning before the train could make its way down the tracks. As the men worked, many of the women passengers helped make and distribute hot drinks as well as pass out and share whatever meager snacks they could locate on the train or from their personal belongings.

At one point in the night, when Donovan was taking a break, the young woman who had spoken out earlier passed by with a tray of crackers and a pot of hot tea. Donovan had since learned that her last name was Marston.

"Thank you, ma'am," Lucas said as she poured him a cup of hot tea.

"Vicki," she replied.

"I beg your pardon?"

"My name is Victoria Marston. My friends call me Vicki."

The Mountie nodded. He had known other women before, but none had ever had the ability to make him feel so inept and tongue-tied. "Thanks," he managed to finally get out. "I'm Lucas. Corporal Lucas Donovan at your service."

The woman laughed aloud. "Pardon me," she said, a little flustered. "But I'm always tickled by how polite all you Canadians are."

"You aren't from around here?" Lucas asked, surprised.

She shook her head. "Yankee, born and bred."

Donovan just smiled and shrugged his shoulders, trying hard to think of something to keep the conversation going. "So, how'd you come to be on the train? I mean, that is, if you don't mind my asking?"

"Why would I?" Vicki replied, smiling. "After all, you just saved my life, and, as far as I know, I'm not under investigation by the North-West Mounted Police."

"Well, I don't know about that. I could start questioning you right now ...," Donovan declared with a smile, starting to feel a little more comfortable.

"Well, well, so, he's finally coming out of his shell," she remarked with a sly grin. "If you must know, I was visiting my sister-in-law. Now I'm returning to my home back in the States.

"Sister-in-law," Lucas repeated, admittedly a little let down. He gulped down the tea.

"My brother's wife," Vicki explained. "I was staying with her while he was away on a job."

"Oh, your brother's ... um ... so ... good. So, well ... I'm heading down to the States myself," Lucas offered, relieved that she might not be married.

"Well, maybe we'll get a chance to learn a little more about each other on the trip," Vicki replied encouragingly. She held out the tray, so he could place the empty cup on it. "If we ever get going again, that is."

"I'd like that," Lucas said, then his mind went blank for several moments. As she started to step away, he said rather too loudly: "And thanks for the tea." Again, he was at a loss for words, so he smiled, picked up his shovel, and stated the obvious: "Well, I guess I'd better get back to it. The snow isn't going to shovel itself."

Vicki looked back at all the men shoveling snow off the tracks. "You are absolutely right, Corporal Donovan." She smiled at the young Mountie, and then headed off to the shelter of the train.

It was near noon when the engineer and the crew agreed that enough snow had been cleared from the tracks and that they had enough steam to get the train rolling again. The crew and passengers returned to the train, and the sled dogs were put in one of the spare cars.

Several hours later they arrived at the next station, where there would be a two-hour layover before the train headed south again, down toward the border crossing.

Lucas arranged with the stationmaster to shelter his dog team, and then sent word to the fort that the team was ready to be picked up the next time someone with the force was in the area. The station-master was able to accommodate the animals in the dog houses at the back of the building. Donovan also reported that the railroad's stationmaster had assured him that, given the circumstances, the railroad company would be happy to make good on a replacement sled and anything else of importance that had been destroyed.

With that, Donovan boarded the train with the red and white malamute by his side. He moved from the first passenger car to the next, hoping to find Miss Victoria Marston with an available seat beside her.

CHAPTER TWELVE

With all the snow, it was a full two-day trip down to the border crossing, but as far as Corporal Lucas Donovan was concerned, time seemed to be going by much too quickly. Red didn't seem to mind the journey. If he wasn't asleep in the middle of the aisle, blocking the flow of passengers, he was playfully pacing back and forth among the passengers, wagging his tail and enjoying the attention he received as he moved from one end of the car to the other.

As was to be expected with two young and attractive people, both Lucas and Vicki passed the time together, making small talk—mostly having to do with the landscape, the weather, or general news of the day.

Eventually, Victoria inquired about his family, whether he had any brothers or sisters. Lucas became solemn and looked out the window. Immediately she knew she had said something wrong or asked something too personal. "I'm sorry ...," she stuttered, "if I ... you don't have to tell me, if you don't want to."

"You needn't apologize. It's just that I recently lost my brother and I miss him."

"I am so sorry, Lucas," Victoria said, placing her hand tentatively on his arm. "Sincerely, I am. If it's not too painful, and you feel like talking about it, I'm a good listener."

Lucas looked at her and tried to smile. "Painful? What was painful was how we lost him. But my memories of Jamie are all good."

"What was he like?" she asked.

"Well, for one thing we were identical twins, so obviously he was incredibly handsome," he joked, trying to make Vicki feel comfortable. And to make himself feel better, too.

"No doubt," Vicki responded, then smiled.

"We were different in many ways. He was older than me by twenty minutes, something he never let me forget. He was more of a thinker, if you know what I mean. He always wanted to study things, think carefully and methodically before moving ahead. And he was a better tracker than I was." Lucas paused and smiled. "You could always count on him to be there when you needed him. No matter what was going on."

Vicki looked into Lucas' eyes. "I suspect if he were asked, he would have said the same thing about you. So how did he die?"

Lucas fidgeted in his seat and took a deep breath and decided he would tell her. "He was a Mountie, too ... like me. The two of us were on the trail of an evil man in the back country, and Jamie and I were bushwhacked. You know, shot from hiding. I was hit, too, but just grazed. He was buried with full honors a few days ago." Lucas realized he didn't want to talk about Jamie's death, especially with a virtual stranger, even if she was a very beautiful stranger. "I'm sorry, but can we please change the subject?"

"Of course. I understand completely," Vicki said.

They both stared out the window, watching the falling snow. Donovan fell asleep for an hour. When he awoke, Vicki was still sitting beside him.

When she realized he was awake, she said very quickly: "So tell me about Red. Where in the world did you find such a noble beast?"

At the sound of his name, the big malamute let out a bark and trotted over. The pair both started laughing, even though they didn't really know why.

* * * * *

At least as far as Lucas was concerned, the time he spent with Vicki Marston was much too brief. But her presence was creating a dilemma for him. His opportunities to spend time with the female persuasion had been few and far between since grade school. He knew what he had to do, but he wanted to do something else. That something else was to follow Miss Marston, wherever she was going.

When Lucas got off the train with Red, he gave a hand to the young woman who had made a big impression on him in a very short time. As he prepared to say goodbye to her, she said she wanted to get off the train and walk around for a bit.

"I have to say I have enjoyed our time together, Miss Marston," Donovan said.

"Canadians ... always so polite," she said, shaking her head. "I told you to call me Vicki, remember?"

Lucas nodded back with a grin. "Vicki it is then."

"So, I take it you're not continuing on by train?" she commented.

"No, sadly I'm not. I need to get some provisions here in town, and then I'll be traveling cross country by horse. But, as I was about to say, I would really like to see you again sometime. I don't know if that would be possible, but it's what I would truly like."

Miss Marston tilted her head in an almost coquettish manner and smiled. "Really?" she asked.

Lucas blushed a second time in her presence. Red looked up at him curiously and barked. "I mean, um ... yes, of course I would like to continue our acquaintance. It's just that I have pressing obligations that may take me ... well, I don't actually know where," he stammered.

Vicki Marston laughed aloud. "Of course, I'd like to see you again as well. Everyone knows where my family lives if you decide to come to Helena. That's in Montana. If you find the time, of course. Just don't take too long."

Lucas was both taken aback and enthralled by the unabashed directness of this bold young lady. "I won't. But I don't exactly know how long it will take, my … business … but I will do all I can to resolve it quickly."

Vicki Marston looked at the tall Canadian as if she were sizing him up for the very first time. "You mentioned that your brother was a Mountie as well, and that he was killed in the line of duty. This pressing obligation of yours … it wouldn't have something to do with that, would it?"

She knew immediately by the look on his face that she should never have asked him this question, but she felt so at ease with him, she couldn't help but be open with him.

"I shouldn't have asked you that," she said, clearly uncomfortable. Despite his reaction to her question, she said: "Well, Lucas Donovan, you go get your business done, but be careful. From the little you've told me, I don't believe your quest will be an easy one, and I'm not fond of the idea of you getting hurt. Or worse yet, never seeing you again."

Knowing he had to get moving, Lucas replied firmly: "Oh, you'll see me again, I assure you."

"And be sure to take care of Red for me, won't you?" Vicki added with a big smile, then she blew Lucas a kiss, and hurried back into the train station.

Donovan shook his head in wonderment and watched her disappear into the crowd.

* * * * *

The border town wasn't very big, only a dozen buildings or so, but there was a general store, a livery stable, and two saloons. He could get the supplies he needed, including what he had lost in his downhill run to save the train, a horse, and perhaps, if he were lucky, some useful information.

Lucas knew that whatever the town size or location, a local saloon was always the best place to hear the local gossip. Lips that are wet with beer are usually loose, he reasoned, and he had a number of questions that needed answers. For the moment, however, that would have to wait. After getting a sufficient amount of gold out of his money belt where no eyes could see him, Donovan picked up his Sharps rifle and his bedroll pack and headed over to the livery stable, Red faithfully trotting right alongside.

The stable was a large lean-to affair with a pine-log corral out front. Inside the corral were a dozen or so geldings and a few mares. For the most part, the mares looked older, and in Donovan's opinion had been, as the old saying goes, "ridden hard, and put away wet."

Lucas ordered Red into a "down and stay" position as he studied the horses. The dog had grown up around horses and was not spooked or even particularly interested in them. Malamutes are sled dogs, not herding dogs. A collie on the other hand, would have immediately busied itself trying to bunch the herd up tighter.

Soon enough, an old man with a long and salt-and-pepper beard came out from the back and approached Lucas. "Seen you admiring this fine stock of mine. Interested in purchasing one, perhaps?" he asked.

"Perhaps, depending on the price," Lucas replied. "But I get to see them all, and then take my pick."

The older man nodded. "Shore, shore, no problem. Around here, the price is always negotiable, but o' course it will depend on which one you pick. They's all prime, that's for shore, but some is better than others."

"These the only ones you've got?" Donovan asked, then added: "Anyone else in town selling?"

The proprietor looked insulted. "Sonny boy, iffen they's any better than mine around here, they shore as shootin' won't be for sale. Now you want to pick one or not?"

Before the owner had shown up, a black gelding in the pen

had caught Donovan's eye. It was mule eared, meaning that it held its two ears sideways, like a mule, rather than straight up. People often look down upon horses with this particular characteristic, but Lucas' father had raised one once, and it was one of the best horses he'd ever ridden. How the animal held its ears might make him look funny to most, but Lucas knew it had absolutely no effect on the horse's hearing or any other trait necessary in a good riding horse.

The black also looked like it might have some Morgan blood in it, and Lucas favored that rare breed. He had no doubt that the animal was all horse, but, still, he wanted to make sure that he made the best possible purchase. After all, it wasn't called horse trading for nothing.

Donovan wanted a mount that would go the distance cross country without breaking down. He liked his horses trail-wise, spirited, and sound. Color and ear carriage meant nothing to him. Of course, he chuckled to himself, this owner didn't need to know all that.

"Sure, let's have a look at them," Donovan answered the man, and they entered the corral. For the next half hour, he examined each horse, keeping his eye on the black, but paying close attention to the legs and hoofs of each and every one of the horses. He recalled what he had heard plenty of horsemen say over the years—"No feet, no horse."—and the Donovans always took that sage advice very seriously.

"Nice gray one over here," the liveryman offered eagerly.

"You mean the one with shin splints and those quarter cracks over his hoofs? No thanks," Donovan replied, shaking his head. He spent some time looking over a big chestnut mare. After looking at her teeth, Lucas dismissed her. As he neared the black, he glanced around the pen, as though he wasn't interested in the horse. Keeping his eye fixed across the pen, he asked: "How much for the chestnut mare, or maybe that buckskin gelding over there?"

The liveryman rubbed his beard while considering his chances at selling a horse or two to this tall stranger. "Well, I might let either one of them go for a hundred dollars cash … each."

The price wasn't unreasonable for a horse in fairly sound condition, but neither of these two fit the bill. Donovan was just trying to get a feel for the man's prices.

"Hmm, I don't know. I'm not sure yet." He then pretended to notice the big black for the first time. "What's this? He half mule? Will you just look at those ears?" He stood there with his hands on his hips and let out a loud laugh. Lucas walked around the horse, looked quickly inside its mouth, then backed off as if this was the last horse on earth he would consider buying.

Lucas was a little surprised at what he had discovered about the black. The teeth indicated the gelding to be only about five years old and that he had a nice, even bite. He was also pleased that the black clearly wasn't a wood cribber or a wind sucker, traits that can ruin a horse. After all, he knew that biting and chewing on wood, or clamping down and sucking wind are vices that some stabled animals develop. Those traits can lead to feeding disorders and colic. An experienced horseman can detect either problem if the horse's teeth are excessively worn down or if the bite line has gaps or is crooked.

The old man looked embarrassed, but the salesman in him wouldn't allow him to give ground.

"Well I'll admit he ain't much to look at, but he's ... er ... young and strong," the man pointed out.

"And probably stupid and stubborn as a jack," Lucas added, not slowing down his criticisms of the horse he really wanted. He ran his hands down the horse's legs, confirming what he already expected, that the animal was both sound and strong.

"Why is this mule-eared one even for sale?" Lucas asked dismissively.

"Well, sir, looks ain't everything, 'specially in a horse."

"Yeah, well, in this case you got that right. Still, I might be able to use him as a backup, if the price is right."

"Well, I know for a fact he rides real comfortable," the liveryman said.

"Really?" Lucas tried to act surprised.

"Fact is, the man who sold me this lot of horses said he'll go all day and all night without a hitch. No quit in him I was told."

"And you believed him? This the same man who was trying to sell you all his stock?"

"Believe him? Yes, sir, I did," the old man answered. He seemed to be getting annoyed.

Although Lucas had no doubt about the horse's stamina, he shook his head anyway. "Maybe if the mule in him don't get in the way. Well, let's see, you want a hundred apiece for those other ones, but I'm tight on funds. So, I'll tell you what, I'll give you thirty-five in gold for this black, and twenty-five for that buckskin over there to use as a pack horse."

"Beggars can't be choosers, huh?" the man rubbed his face for a moment, not wanting to look too anxious to sell either of the horses. "Nope. For the two o' them … let's say hundred fifty dollars is the best I can do, unless maybe you want to throw in that big ol' dog o' yours?"

"No, sir," Donovan said hastily, "he's not for sale, but thanks for the offer." Lucas reached into his pockets and tipped back on the heels of his boots, pretending to think about the price.

"One fifty, huh? Well, I'll tell you what. In that case, things being as slim as they are, I guess I'll have to split the difference with you. I offered sixty for both and you want one hundred fifty, so how about I take the bay mule and the buckskin for the same thirty-five each."

The liveryman rubbed his beard, cocking an eyebrow at Donovan. He knew how hard it would be to unload that mule-ear for a decent price, but he also remembered how much he'd paid for the whole lot and he needed to recoup his costs at the least. The man shook his head. "Nope, sorry, sonny, but I can't go down that low. And besides, he ain't a mule. Shore you don't wanna sell that dog?"

After his examination of the horse, Donovan would gladly have paid a full hundred for the big black horse alone, ears or no ears. He reached into his pocket and counted out seventy in gold. "Nope, not for sale, and this is all I will pay. If you're not amenable to the deal, maybe you can sell them to a trapper who's hard up for something cheap to eat."

The liveryman bristled at the remark. "Yeah? And then what would you ride?" he said. The old man looked back at the black, who was munching on some hay. That downward position made his floppy ears seem even larger. The horse trader shook his head in despair. "Eighty dollars fer both and that's final."

"Fine. Eighty dollars it is," Donovan replied as he reached into his pocket where he had put one hundred in coins earlier. But then he dropped his hand, saying: "I'll need a bill of sale and I want them shod before I leave."

"Cost you extra," the old codger continued to dicker.

Lucas jingled the coins in his hand and shook his head firmly. "Oh, no, it won't, not for a half mule who's probably not even worth the thirty-five and a run-down pack horse."

"Fine, you win. Come back in two hours, and they'll be ready."

Lucas handed the man the forty dollars. The liveryman looked puzzled. "You'll get the rest after I check the new horseshoes myself," Donovan explained.

"Sonny, you shore do drive a hard bargain. You shore you never ran a livery yourself?"

Donovan laughed and patted the bay horse. "I think I'll call him Handsome Harry. See you in two hours. Thanks, mister."

"Yeah, right," the old man mumbled angrily.

CHAPTER THIRTEEN

"Next stop, the general store," Donovan said to Red. "Come on, boy." Red's ears perked up, and he bounded after his master.

"No sense having a horse without a saddle, now is there?" Lucas said aloud to the dog. He found what he was looking for at the end of the street. The rolls of barbed wire and the assorted shovels and brooms leaning against the wall outside the door were a dead giveaway.

The sign above the door read: NORTHERN SUPPLY COMPANY. It didn't look big enough to be an actual company, so Lucas surmised that it might be part of a conglomerate of small stores owned by some rich banker, back east, maybe. On the other hand, it could be that the store owner was merely trying to make his place sound more important than it was in actuality.

There were two men leaving the store just as Donovan walked in; another was finishing up at the counter, counting out his money. The place seemed typical of almost any small town general store. It was rectangular and long. Hundreds of items hung down from the ceiling on hooks or wires. There were lariats, lamps, canteens hanging from their straps, and just about anything else that could be strung up. A long wooden counter stretched down along the side of the store, and behind it were dozens of little cubbyholes filled with things like tobacco jars, cigars, all kinds of candies, boxes of bullets, and other assorted small items.

Behind the counter stood a middle-aged, balding man in a white shirt and a black bow tie. At the moment, he was looking impatient as the man slowly counted out his money, starting over several times.

Toward the back of the store, just past some tables that had clothing laid out on them, were a few wooden sawhorses with new saddles thrown over them. There were a few older saddles in a pile on the floor next to them.

Donovan had always loved stores like these. As a kid, he would stare at the glass jars full of jawbreakers, sticks of licorice, and lollipops, and hope that his father would have a couple of pennies left over for his two sons.

Now, as an adult, he still enjoyed slowly perusing the aisles of such stores, looking for some new kind of gadget that he might never have seen before. He recalled the first time he saw an apple peeler. A traveling salesman was demonstrating it to the store owner, and Lucas and Jamie had watched in fascination as the salesman stuck an apple on a small spike in the center of the device. He lowered the cupped top, which held the apple in place, and then began turning a hand crank that was located on the side of the peeling device. The customers in the store at the time, both women and men, let out little *ahhs* as they watched the apple turn. In no time at all, the sharp blade had peeled the skin off the whole apple, leaving it intact, but naked as Adam and Eve. The store owner had ordered five of them on the spot. Several women stepped up to put in an order, thinking how much time they could save when making apple pies and wondering if there were other fruits and vegetables they could use with the newfangled machine.

Lucas smiled at the memory and headed to the back of the store, toward the pile of saddles on the floor.

"Don't much like dogs in my store," the clerk behind the counter said firmly. Red growled in answer to his comment.

"Behave, Red," Lucas commanded. He walked the big dog back to the front door and had him sit. "Stay Red." Lucas wagged his finger at the dog for emphasis.

Turning to the store owner, Donovan explained: "If I tied him up outside, he'd just chew through the rope and scratch at your window. I promise he'll behave as long as he can see me."

The clerk didn't seem very convinced.

"I'm looking for a saddle," Lucas added.

"Got some nice new ones over here," the clerk said, as he stepped out from behind the counter. The prospect of a sale of a saddle appeared to suddenly outweigh his concern about the dog.

It wasn't that Lucas couldn't afford a new one or that he was by nature tightfisted. He wasn't. However, what he had learned through the years, is that a new saddle takes a while to break in, during which time the rider's behind suffers the consequences. Furthermore, after the first week or two, a new saddle is no better or worse than an old saddle that has been properly maintained. Good leather will almost last a lifetime, if its cared for by its owner. As far as Lucas was concerned, it made little sense to pay ten times the price for the same long-term value.

Donovan sifted through a couple of saddles, discarding them due to worn out padding, rusted metal, a cracked tree, or degrading leather. The last thing he wanted was to ruin a good horse by causing fistulous withers or an abscessed back from riding with a defective saddle. Lucas was beginning to think he might have to buy a new one, when he turned over a saddle from the bottom of the pile.

To the average Yankee, that saddle might have seemed strange, or perhaps even been confused for a pack saddle, but to a Canadian Mountie it was perfect. At first glance, it appeared to be an altered McClellan Army saddle, named after the Army general who had designed it. Donovan had heard its nickname a number of times—the ballbuster. It differed from the usual roping saddles, or even the English-style saddle used for pleasure riding, in that the center portion of the seat was open, which alleviated the problem of the saddle seat rubbing the horse's back, and was more useful to the cavalry. The US military appeared to appreciate horses more than soldiers.

The saddle Lucas was looking at, however, differed from other McClellans in several ways. This one had two long wooden skis on which the saddle seat rested that were covered with leather. There were also two flat metal bars reaching up from the middle of the skis in a crossed-arm pattern that attached to the bottom of the saddle seat. This raised the seat higher up off the horse than that of a regular saddle. Like the roping saddles from Texas, this saddle also had the wide skirts and fenders that hung down low under the seat to protect the inside of the rider's legs. Two leather straps ran down opposite sides, ending in hooded stirrups, called tapaderos, which are favored by Mexican vaqueros because they keep thorns from penetrating one's shoes and boots when riding the open range. When everything was put together on a saddle like this, the finished product was one highly favored by the Mounties, especially since it was remarkably comfortable.

Pulling the saddle from the pile, Lucas noticed that although it was dusty, the leather was still in great shape and all that was missing was a girth strap. Donovan had noticed that there were plenty of those in the store that would do the job nicely.

"How much you want for this saddle here?" Lucas called to the store clerk. "The dirty one missing the girth strap."

"You want that one? Hell, we got several new ones that are much nicer," the clerk, suddenly a salesman, pointed out. "I got that off of a Canuck who passed through here. Never seen one south o' the border. No decent rider'd be caught dead on it. Looks uncomfortable as hell. Probably tear your arse a new hole." He walked over and pointed out a San Antonio roper. "Now this one's pretty solid and a lot more comfortable. At a hundred dollars, it's a real bargain."

Donovan bristled at the man's use of the term *Canuck*, a

disparaging term used by Americans when referring to Canadians—a northern version of the term gringo. On any other occasion
Donovan might have raised a ruckus over the insult, but today
Lucas decided to let it go. The clerk was obviously ignorant, not
having caught the Mountie's slight accent, and Donovan wanted a
good deal on the used saddle.

"Well, that's fine if you want to spend a hundred," Lucas said,
"but I don't. This one here's pretty dirty and beat up, but the leather
seems intact, so I figure it'll be cheap enough for me. I'll give you
twenty dollars."

The clerk considered the offer for a moment before replying:
"Twenty-five."

"Deal, if you throw in a girth strap to replace the one that's
missing."

The clerk scratched his head as he considered Donovan's offer.
"You're a Can … Canadian, aren't you?" he said. "Didn't mean to
insult you. But most folks call them cinches down here in the States,
not girth straps."

"We got a deal?" Donovan asked, ignoring the fact the clerk had
made an attempt at an apology. "Think about it, because I also need
a bridle and a few other items."

The clerk nodded. "Sure. I figure I can make it up on the rest of
the stuff you need, anyway." He smiled hesitantly at Donovan, and
held out his hand, introducing himself: "Holly Glunn."

Lucas took his hand and introduced himself. He was sort of
taking a liking to the man.

It took another half an hour for Lucas to purchase the other
supplies that he needed. While in the store, he changed into another
shirt, this one a red flannel checked, and a pair of denim pants in a
style becoming more popular of late.

Just before leaving, Lucas stopped by a rack of new hats. He
tried on a cattleman-style Stetson, grinning when he looked in the
mirror that was hanging on the wall near the rack.

"Lookin' mighty fine in that hat," Holly commented. "Right smart I'd say. I can make you a good price on it, too."

Donovan looked down at his broad-brimmed felt campaign hat with its symmetrically pinched high crown, and let out a sigh. *Once a Mountie, always a Mountie I guess,* he thought to himself.

"No thanks, I think I'll just stick with this one," he told the clerk.

"Too bad. You look like a real cowboy in that. Anything else I can do for you?" Holly asked, a hopeful look on his face.

Lucas shook his head and started to pay him, but stopped. "Wait, there is one thing more. Might you hold the saddle and these supplies while I go get my horses?"

Since Donovan was going to pay in gold, rather than ask for credit, Mr. Glunn cheerfully agreed. "No problem. We're open till six o'clock tonight, or as long as I need to be. And we open early in the morning, if you need to leave your things overnight."

"Right thoughtful of you. I might just do that," Lucas said, and added: "Thanks much, Mister Glunn."

Because Donovan figured it would still be a while before his horses were ready, he left the store, and went looking for the town sheriff, Red following happily behind.

CHAPTER FOURTEEN

When Donovan entered the sheriff's office, he was surprised by its filthy condition. Even in the most remote Canadian outposts, the NWMP constables always tried to maintain a clean living and working environment.

This office had on its floor a good portion of the dirt that should have been out on the street. The sound of Donovan's boot heels was muffled by the dirt as he stepped in and closed the door. In the middle of the room, a large desk took up most of the space, and, behind it, a rather round middle-aged man snored loudly. His boots were perched atop the desk, his hat pulled down over his eyes. His legs appeared to be short, so he wasn't a tall man.

The Mountie took a moment to look around. There was a Stevens double-barreled shotgun propped in one corner. A quick glance indicated that, like the office, it wasn't well maintained. The stove held a pot of coffee, but the pot was so dirty on the outside, he knew he wouldn't accept a cup, if offered. Alongside the stove was a large pegboard with some keys hanging on it. Lucas assumed they were for the jail cells in the back.

Donovan stepped back, opened the door, and slammed it shut loudly. The startled lawman woke up, swinging his feet off the desk and jumping up. The speed in which he accomplished this feat took Donovan by surprise. Nonetheless, the sheriff seemed briefly disoriented before he realized there was a stranger in his office. After giving Lucas the once over, he relaxed some.

"Can I help you?" he asked.

Donovan reached into his pocket.

"Whoa, easy there, stranger," the sheriff said as he stood up. "Take 'er slow." The lawman's hand shifted quickly down to his pistol's grip. He might be slovenly, but apparently the sheriff was experienced and nobody's fool.

"Just reaching for my badge, Sheriff. No need to worry," Donovan said in a reassuring tone.

"Badge, huh?" Well, go on, let's see 'er." The lawman's hand still rested on his gun.

Donovan pulled out his badge. "I'm a corporal with the North-West Mounted Police. Lucas Donovan."

The sheriff glanced at the badge with its insignia, nodded, and seemed to relax. "That so? Huh, what do you know about that? All the way down here." He stuck his hand out, smiling. "Joe Perkins is the name. So, whatcha doin' down here, Corporal? A little out of your territory, ain't you?"

"Just trying to find out some information, Sheriff, nothing more. I'm looking to learn all I can about a man named Emerson. Jack Emerson. Ever heard of him?"

Sheriff Perkins sat down on the edge of his desk and indicated a chair to Donovan. "Light," he invited. The image of a barn-sour horse, one who doesn't like leaving his stall, immediately crossed Donovan's mind when looking at Perkins.

"Friend or foe?" Perkins asked.

"Definitely not my friend," Lucas replied.

"You hunting this fella? You ain't got any jurisdiction down here, you know. That is unless you got some sort of official paper-work ... what the hell am I talking about?"

"No, no papers, Sheriff Perkins. I don't intend to arrest him. If it comes to that here in your town, I'd let you know. If it's somewhere else, I'll be sure to include local law enforcement."

"If it comes to that, huh?" Sheriff Perkins mumbled. "What's he wanted for? Must be big … you comin' all the way down 'cross the border and all for this here feller with no government papers on you?"

Perkins might be short and sloppy, but he's no idiot, Lucas thought, then explained: "Robbery. Murder. Rape. Name a law you can break, and Emerson has broken it."

"So how is it you Mounties let him get out of Canada? What with him being so bad and all?"

"Don't know as we did. I am more of an unofficial scout for the force. I'm down here to make sure we aren't wasting our time searching up in the provinces," Donovan lied. He was counting on this lawman not checking up on him with the Canadian authorities.

"Well, in that case, I'll try to help you out." The sheriff opened one of the desk drawers. "Let's see what we can come up with. That name don't mean nothin' to me personally, but I got a book right here in my desk with all the wanted posters that have been put out over the last couple of years. I sort of collect them. I never throw anythin' out," the lawman commented, which made Donovan smile as he looked at the clutter all around the office.

After a half hour of searching through a stack of posters and drinking what had to be the worst cup of coffee Lucas had ever tasted, the two men failed to come up with a wanted poster for Emerson, or even anyone fitting his description.

"Well, thank you for your help anyway, Sheriff," Donovan said as he wiped his gritty fingers on the legs of his pants. "I did hear that he might have relatives over somewhere on the Montana and Idaho border. A place named Willard Creek. I guess I'll head out that way." Donovan stood.

"They call it Bannack now," the lawman stated, and started tapping the desk and looking at the ceiling as if trying to remember something. Suddenly he snapped his fingers. "Got it. The bartender over at the Busted Flush Saloon is from that area. Name of MacGregor. You might have a talk with him and see if he recognizes the name."

"Thank you, Sheriff. Can I repay the favor and buy you a drink? You can introduce me to this MacGregor."

The lawman thought a moment, but then shook his head. "Like to join you, but I'm still on duty. I'll just stay right here."

He's definitely barn sour, Lucas thought to himself as he left the office.

CHAPTER FIFTEEN

"Next stop, the local watering hole, Red," Lucas said as he took in the fresh air outside the lawman's den. The big malamute cocked his head and then wagged his tail furiously. The pair ambled down the plank walkway to the Busted Flush, located on the same side of the street. It was a rather large building with two floors. As was common with most saloons, there were two wide, batwing doors at the entrance.

"You know the drill, Red. Stay right here." Lucas made a downward motion with the palm of his hand. Red whimpered slightly, but stayed as commanded. But as soon as Lucas entered the saloon, Red inched forward so he could stick his nose far enough into the room to keep an eye on his master.

Donovan stopped right after entering and took in the room in one quick sweep. It was an old habit with him, what gamblers referred to as "reading the room." He noted the location of windows, doors, tables, and occupants—of which there were not that many at the present time. After years on the force, he'd gotten to a point where he could usually detect hideout weapons such as shoulder holsters, sleeve guns, or even hidden knives. Men carrying concealed weapons didn't realize that they often position their bodies in subtle ways to compensate for the shape or weight of the hidden weapon they are carrying. Others make the mistake of too-often patting or touching their clothes to assure themselves the hidden weapons are at the ready or haven't shifted. Such things can be read by the trained eye, with practice.

After reassuring himself that nothing seemed out of the ordinary for a frontier saloon, he walked over to the bar, leaned his Sharps rifle up against it, and waited. A very large man with a full red beard walked over and wiped down the counter in front of him.

"What'll it be, stranger?" he asked. His tone was neither friendly nor hostile. He seemed more bored than anything else.

"You are named MacGregor, are you not?" Lucas asked.

The big barkeep nodded suspiciously, keeping his eye solidly on Donovan.

"I'd like a large ale and some information, if you have any."

"Ale? You mean beer?" the bartender asked, shaking his head with a smirk. He looked Lucas over carefully. "So then, you'd be Canadian, and if I can still see straight, you'd also be a lawman."

"I'm a lawman up in Alberta," Donovan assured him, "but I'm looking for information about a man who might be from a place called Willard Creek, in Idaho, I believe. Sheriff Perkins said you might be able to help. I'd gladly pay for your troubles."

The big man smiled. "Grasshopper Creek? I lived there for a while."

"Grasshopper Creek?" Lucas said, not understanding the connection.

"Well, let's see," the large man began. "Two explorers, Lewis and Clark, originally discovered the place and named it Willard Creek. It was back in the old Idaho Territory. Not much there at the time. You know ... hot in the summer, cold in the fall, and wet and miserable all the time. Sometime later, somebody struck gold there and the place suddenly grew up. Problem was, the whole place was overrun with grasshoppers."

"Grasshoppers? The insects?" Lucas asked.

"Right. Thousands of 'em. They were everywhere. Your ears,

your mouth and eyes, bed sheets, boots, your food, you name it. So the locals began calling the place Grasshopper Creek. Over time, they managed to burn most of them out, and then it became part of this lovely state of Montana. Name was changed again. Bannack, this time. Would have been Bannack with an *o*, but as usual the government mucked things up and misspelled the request."

Lucas chuckled. "I see things with the government are as efficient down here as they are back home. If I might ask, how'd you end up in a place like Grasshopper Creek? I mean if my ears don't deceive me, you are Scottish, aren't you?"

"That's right, my lad, as if there was ever any doubt." He chuckled while stroking his thick red beard. "But the question should be how I ended up here in this fine establishment." MacGregor waved his big arm around the saloon.

"All right, I'm listening," Lucas prompted.

"Well, my father was in the distillery business in Glasgow. As a child I practically bathed in whiskey barrels. I left home at fifteen, determined to find a better life here in America."

"A little big to cowboy, I imagine," Lucas joked.

"A mite, yes, but not too big to drive a wagon. I made my way to Chicago, where I worked the stockyards for two whole years. I then came west with a group that traveled back and forth to Chicago. Moving cattle they were. Along the way, we got word of a gold strike in Willard, so I left that group and headed over there, instead."

"Any luck?" Lucas asked.

"At first, yes. I lived there a few years and it worn't too bad … at first. Later, what with the Plummer gang robbing everyone, the crooked card games, and the local ladies, I soon lost everything I had made, little as it be. Started working my way back eastward, but didn't get very far and that's how I finally ended up here, in this small paradise."

"Back to working with the whiskey you had left in your homeland," Lucas observed.

MacGregor shrugged. "Can't argue with the fates, I guess. So, who is this man you are looking for?"

"A fellow by the name of Emerson. Jack Emerson."

The big man's face went suddenly grim. "Friend of yorn?"

Donovan shook his head. "I'll be honest with you, MacGregor. He killed my brother." He stared the big man in the eye, wondering why he had told him the truth. "I need all the help I can get."

The big bartender nodded. "You sure will, if you go after that group. I don't know this particular fellow, but there's a miserable clan of Emersons all around that area. The whole lot of them are meaner than a grizzly bear with a thorn in its paw. Too much inbreeding, if you ask me. They'd as soon slit your throat as say hello."

"Sounds like the man I'm after would fit right in with this group," Donovan said. Lucas dropped five dollars in coin on the bar. "So how do I find this Willard ... I mean this Bannack?"

The bartender studied Donovan while wiping the bar counter off, sliding the money over to his apron pocket. "Well, you might find it with a map, of course, but it can be pretty tough going. Wait a moment," the barman said, hesitating, "I know of a fellow who's a little down on his luck and would probably guide you for a small fee. Problem is ..." He paused to stroke his beard.

"He's not particularly trustworthy?" Lucas finished the sentence for him.

"No, it isn't that," MacGregor replied.

"Then what is it?" Donovan asked.

"Well he's ... indigenous, you know ... an Injun ... and most folks won't have stock with one. Now me ... I don't care what a man is or where he comes from, as long as he's straight with me."

"That's the way I feel," Lucas replied truthfully. "So, where do I find this fellow?"

MacGregor gestured to the back of the saloon. "He's out back stacking barrels and chopping firewood for lunch money. Can't miss him."

Donovan stuck out his hand and the barkeeper took it. Lucas' whole hand practically disappeared inside the big Scot's grip. He then left the bar and gestured for Red to follow.

They walked around the building to the area out back where he found a slender man cutting wood with a long double-bladed ax. He was obviously an Indian, and, given the locale, Lucas thought he might be one of the Sioux nation.

Donovan cleared his throat. "Hello. Do you speak English?" he asked.

The man eyed him carefully, but then kept his attention on the dog.

"Some," the man replied finally, suspiciously.

"Lakota?" Lucas asked.

The man nodded. "Oglala Lakota."

Donovan noted that the man did not put the ax down.

"*Ininiwuk,*" Lucas said, saying the Cree word used to identify themselves. It meant: men, or original people. "Or I should say, I was raised by one," Donovan said in Cree. He had hoped to set the man more at ease.

Although the Cree and the Sioux languages were not identical, they shared linguistic similarities. In fact, before the arrival of the white man, the tribes had crossed into each other's territories. Lucas hoped the man would understand he had nothing but respect for the native people.

The Indian nodded again, even seemed to relax slightly. He set the ax down next to a large beer barrel. "What want with White Bear?" he asked.

"All I need is a guide to take me to Bannack," Lucas replied. "Grasshopper Creek? I was told by MacGregor that you can get me there."

"Is far away. Many days' ride." His face was expressionless.

"I will pay you well," Lucas said in English. He emphasized what he said by using hand signs.

The Indian thought for a moment and grunted: "No have pony."

"I will buy you a pony and pay for your help," Lucas told him. "Both. Are you willing?"

White Bear looked at the man and his big red and white dog. The he shrugged and nodded. "White Bear take, but no go into town. Not that one."

Donovan considered that for a moment and agreed. "Just get me there, and I'll do the rest. It is a deal?"

"Pay before go. Not after." Obviously, the man had learned long ago to distrust white men. *Probably with good reason*, Lucas thought.

"All right, before we leave, I will pay you. But remember, White Bear, I too have been fooled by others before."

The Indian grunted. "By *white eyes*, not by Lakota."

Lucas chuckled. "Well, you got me there."

"When we go?" White Bear asked. He was a man of few words.

"I would like to leave tomorrow," Lucas replied. "After we get you a horse and we get all the supplies loaded up. I'll meet you at the livery stable early, and we'll see about getting that pony." He extended his arm and White Bear shook his hand. Then without another word, the man picked up the ax and went back to chopping wood.

CHAPTER SIXTEEN

Donovan went back to the livery stable to purchase another horse for White Bear, but this time it was the liveryman who got the best of the deal. After all, it was harder to convince the stableman that he was so hard up when Lucas was wanting to buy a third horse.

The two men finally settled on a blue roan that seemed reasonably sound. The gelding had a white star and stripe on its forehead and, from what Lucas could make out from the horse's teeth, was around twelve years old.

The stable owner agreed to have the roan shod by the time they were ready to leave. Since Lucas had just bought three horses from him, the man agreed to stable the horses overnight at no extra charge.

The Mountie finally headed over to what the liveryman described as "the best hotel in town, especially if you consider we only got one."

As was pretty common, when he entered the hotel, the clerk was taken aback by the presence of an enormous red-and-white malamute.

"We don't allow no dogs in our place," he said firmly.

"He's house broke. Won't be any problem," Lucas assured him.

The clerk, a tall thin middle-aged man with a balding hairline thought a moment, but then shook his head. "No, I don't think so."

Donovan pushed the brim of his hat back a little, took some extra coins out of his pocket, and leaned in. "This ought to cover any inconvenience. Besides," he whispered, "if Red thinks you don't like him, he might eat you like he did the last clerk who gave me a hard time."

The big dog looked up and began to yawn. The hotel clerk felt as though he were peering into the open mouth of a fully grown timber wolf. The man reassessed the extra coins on the counter and gave in. "Fine, but keep him in your room. And you gotta pay for any damage he causes," he told Donovan. The clerk tried to sound tough, but failed miserably.

"Don't worry," Lucas said quietly. "He's as gentle as a kitten. When he's not hungry, that is."

"No doubt," the clerk replied nervously. "Have a nice stay."

"Thanks, but we'll be leaving first thing in the morning."

The clerk clearly seemed relieved at that bit of information.

"One thing, however," Lucas added, "he doesn't do well when I'm not around, so, unless you want to feed him in the restaurant, could you arrange to have three large steaks, some potatoes, and a beer sent up to my room?"

As if right on cue, at the mention of steak, Red let out a loud bark. The dog was merely being playful, but a malamute as big as Red was imposing. Donovan watched the color drain from the face of the clerk and suppressed a smile.

Trembling, the clerk placed his hand over his heart, stuttering: "T-two ... um ... three steaks and potatoes to the room. Coming right up."

As he turned to leave, Lucas reminded the clerk: "And a cold beer for me."

"I'm surprised it's not for him, too," the clerk mumbled to himself.

Once settled in his room, Lucas evaluated the progress he was making while Red ate one of the steaks. Donovan ate half a steak and the potatoes. When they were both done eating, the two drifted into a deep sleep—Lucas on the bed and Red right next to the bed, on the floor.

The following morning, Donovan was up with the sunrise. He poured Red some water and gave him the remaining steak he had saved for him, while he ate the other half of his steak he hadn't finished. He washed up in a small bowl provided in the corner and dried himself with a towel—embroidered with a rose pattern—that was draped over the stand that held the ceramic bowl and pitcher. He looked into the mirror and considered shaving, but, wanting to save time, decided he would let it go.

Lucas buckled on his wide leather belt with its cross-draw flapped holster. After checking his pistol, he adjusted his hat and picked up the Sharps rifle that was leaning against the door. Lucas let out a small whistle and the big dog jumped up and followed him out the door.

The pair arrived at the stable just as it was opening. Off to the left of the entrance White Bear was sitting, cross-legged, with his back up against the wall.

"What did you do ... sleep here?" Lucas asked, looking up at the sun. "And I thought I was an early riser," he muttered to himself.

White Bear merely grunted and stood up. "We go now?"

Donovan shook his head. "Got to pick up our saddles and tack and other supplies over at the general store first."

The liveryman led the three horses out of the barn and handed the lead ropes to Lucas. He in turn handed the rope for the blue roan to White Bear. "He okay with you?"

The Indian checked the horse's feet and hoofs, studied him all around. For the first time since they had met, White Bear actually cracked a small smile. "Good."

"Thought you'd like him," Lucas said. "Just don't go all mushy on me with gratitude or anything."

Turning to the liveryman, he asked: "You want the ropes and halters back."

"Naw, keep 'em. They's old ropes, anyhow. Besides, I appreciate a man who knows how to horse trade. Have a safe trip … wherever you're goin'."

Lucas touched the brim of his hat and thanked the man as he and White Bear led the horses down the street to the store where he had left his supplies. As always, Red trotted along happily, stopping only long enough to relieve himself on a nearby post.

"How long you expect this trip will take?" Lucas asked.

White Bear thought a moment before answering. "If no problems, should be there in ten, eleven days."

Donovan considered the answer and grinned. "You expecting trouble, my friend?"

"Things always go right for you?" White Bear asked.

Remembering his brother Jamie, Lucas shook his head. "No, I guess they don't. Leastwise, not lately."

Planning for a trip on horseback, even one expected to last ten days or so, still required forethought. And although it would be prudent not to overburden the animals, Lucas knew he would have to stock up for any number of eventualities, as well as add provisions to accommodate White Bear's needs.

His purchase included tack, saddle blankets, canteens, canned goods, and bedrolls, as well as feedbags and grain for the horses, ammunition for the weapons, a spare set of clothing and extra gloves and socks. Life in the Canadian north had taught Lucas the importance of having warm dry socks on more than one occasion, and he had no reason to believe Montana would be any different, even though there wasn't much snow except in the mountains.

The last things Lucas and White Bear packed away into their pack and saddle bags were a medicine kit, a set of extra horseshoes and nails, a pair of pliers, a rasp, a sharpening stone, a small hand ax, and a box of strike-on-anything matches.

Once the horses were saddled and the pack horse had been fitted with a long lead rope, the men rode out of town, west toward the town of Bannack.

CHAPTER SEVENTEEN

That first day, the pair made good time. The weather was cool and dry, and the horses seemed to enjoy being out and away from that crowded corral.

The pair made about twenty miles before stopping for the night. On the trail, horses can travel twice that distance per day, but faster speeds tend to wear them out sooner and can quickly ruin a good animal. Lucas knew Pony Express riders averaged ten miles per hour, but they switched horses every twenty-five miles or so. Only by changing horses frequently could riders routinely cover eighty to one hundred miles per day.

When they stopped to make camp for the night, White Bear set about gathering wood and making a fire. Lucas broke out the tins and utensils and cooked up a sort of prairie stew, using some beans, a potato, and a plump squirrel that White Bear had shot just as they were riding into camp. Considering he was using an old Starr carbine, Lucas was impressed with the Lakota's shooting ability.

Over dinner, White Bear was his usual closed-mouth self. On the trail Lucas could have counted all the words the man had spoken on two hands and still have a finger or two to spare.

"A lady likes to be appreciated for her cooking, you know?" the Mountie joked as they were finishing up.

"I am eating it, no? Good enough," White Bear replied.

After a minute or so, he looked up from his plate. "Not my business, but wonder why white man want go to Bannack?" he asked.

Lucas picked up the coffee pot, using a doubled-over glove to keep from getting burned, and poured himself and his companion a cup. He hesitated before answering.

"I am a Canadian Mounted Policeman. Do you know what that is?"

White Bear nodded, but remained expressionless as he answered: "Pony soldier. Wear red coat."

"That's right. Don't have mine on now, but I am a Mountie. So you know of us?"

"When the Lakota fought and killed Yellow Hair …," White Bear started to say.

"Yellow Hair? You mean General Custer?" Lucas interrupted.

White Bear just grunted. "After battle our people had hard time. Army chase and kill many. After a year, Sitting Bull finally led our people across the white man's border to the north."

"I remember that," Donovan commented.

"Sioux and Blackfeet end up in same land. Latoka and Blackfeet dogs not friends. Big problem about to happen when a pony soldier, named Walsh, rode into our camp."

"James Morrow Walsh. I know the name. That was near the Wood Mountain area, wasn't it?" Donovan asked.

"Yes. Pony Soldier Walsh come into camp of many Lakota with just a guide. Sitting Bull see bravery in this man right off."

Donovan nodded and smiled. "James Walsh is a legend among his own people."

"Walsh stop trouble between Blackfeet and my people. Later, when an Assiniboine start trouble in camp, Pony Soldier Walsh stop him and fix trouble all by himself. Sitting Bull so happy, he make friends with Walsh and told our people to obey the Queen Mother's laws. Walsh good man."

"My brother was a ... pony soldier, too," Lucas explained. "He was killed a while back. He was bushwhacked ... you understand? ... Shot by an outlaw from hiding. Bushwhacker shot at me, too. I am looking for that man."

The Indian sipped his coffee and seemed to contemplate what Donovan had told him before saying anything. Finally, looking Lucas straight in the eye, he said: "You good man, and White Bear understand blood oath, but I still no go into Bannack."

"I know ... you've told me," Lucas said. "Why is that exactly?"

White Bear nodded. "I will make sure you get there. Made promise to you. But no go into town. Is bad place for White Bear. After Sitting Bull took tribe back south to raise white flag, we thought peace made. But not so. White men still see us as enemy. One day when White Bear took wife and child to white man's town, he was hit on head, hard. The men who did it thought White Bear dead, but was wrong. When I come awake, my woman and son dead. He was only small, small boy."

"I am truly sorry," Lucas said, feeling like he swallowed a rock.

"No one want to help Sioux, so I took my family away. Buried them in hills. I have fought the *white eyes* and won, but lost my family. No more. No go into that town. White Bear will keep promise and take you there, but I no go in that Bannack."

"I understand, my friend," Donovan reassured White Bear. "I have no intention of making you a part of my troubles. Just get me to Bannack as fast as possible, and I will always consider that my friend did his job well."

"White Bear not afraid."

"Never entered my mind that you were," Lucas said in all sincerity.

"No want other peoples' troubles. Just want to live life. What left of it," the Sioux explained.

"And for that, I don't blame you. Your life, your rules," Lucas replied. "Like I said, just get me to Bannack and we're square."

White Bear simply nodded and set down his tin cup. "Good food. Good company. Bad coffee."

* * * * *

Over the next several days the men rode along, putting more miles behind them. Donovan took in the country, appreciating the openness and beauty. The mountains, rolling hills, wooded areas, and the wide-open expanses of land that were breathtaking. Sadly, the panoramic landscape could not totally distract him from his mission, one that would not end well either for himself or Emerson.

"How much longer?" the Mountie asked the Lakota guide.

"Six more days maybe. We reach small town in one day, if you want buy more supplies, or rest."

"Might not be a bad idea. Maybe get a beer and take a bath," Lucas said.

The Indian looked at him, perplexed. Neither of the two things Donovan had mentioned had entered White Bear's mind as something to do in a town.

A day and a half later, around noon time, the pair rode into the town of Elk Grove. There wasn't an elk in sight. *Maybe there were herds of the animal here when the town was first settled,* Lucas thought to himself, wondering how they came up with town names south of the border.

As they rode past the livery, Lucas stopped and nodded to White Bear. "Do me a favor and see if we can get the horses stabled for a while. Maybe grain them a little extra, too." He reached over and handed some coins to his companion.

"Where you go?" the Lakota asked somewhat anxiously.

"I'm going to find out where the sheriff's office is. I want to head over there and have a word with him. Give me about a half hour, and then I will meet you out in front of that saloon over there." Donovan pointed down the street as he dismounted, then handed his reins to White Bear.

The Sioux nodded, took the reins, and turned the horses to the livery with some apprehension. He did not like being in a town full of *white eyes* he didn't know. In his experience, members of his tribe were not received well in such places. Besides, he always thought that the towns of the white men carried a bad smell in the air.

Lucas walked down the street, Red following closely, and before long he found the town jail. He opened the door, only to find the front room empty. "Anyone home?" he called out.

A tall thin man in his midthirties came into the office from the back where the jail cells would be located. He carried a broom in his hand, and, after sweeping a small pile of dirt out of the doorway, he turned. He took one look at the malamute and promptly jumped back and held out the broom as if to ward off the animal.

"He won't bite," Lucas said, as he signaled the dog to sit.

"Won't bite, eh? Probably just swallows you whole," the lawman said.

Lucas chuckled. "Not to worry, Sheriff, he's already had his fill today. I'm looking for a little information."

The lawman looked him up and down suspiciously.

"Information about what?" he leaned the broom against the wall and went to his desk.

"My name is Donovan. Lucas Donovan, and I'm looking for a man named Emerson. Jack Emerson."

The sheriff paused a moment as if startled, but he quickly regained his composure. "My name's Jefferson. Pete Jefferson," he said, and extended his hand toward Donovan over the desk. They shook hands, and the sheriff indicated that Lucas should take a seat. Red yawned loudly and stretched out on the floor in front of the door.

Jefferson gathered up the papers on his desk and moved them into a drawer. "Emerson, you say?" he said. "So what's this fellow done that you'd be asking about him in a sheriff's office?"

"Well, sir, I'm not sure if he's actually done anything in your town, but the Mounties are looking for him for some killings up across the border," Donovan explained.

"They ain't got no jurisdiction down here, you know."

"No, of course not," Lucas replied. "I just came down here to determine if he is here in the States or not."

"You got some sort of special paperwork on him?" the sheriff asked. "Gonna try and take him back?"

"Oh, no, nothing like that. I'm off duty down here, but I thought I could save the government some money and manpower by determining whether he had actually crossed the border. No sense in looking for someone in your country, if he's left it." Donovan hoped his explanation sounded convincing.

"Since when does the government ever worry about wasting money?" Lucas laughed in agreement. "That's a fact, but I can tell you that my superiors worry a lot about money."

"So you're a Mountie then," the lawman said, stating the obvious.

Donovan nodded. "Yes, sir, but as you pointed out, I'm acting on behalf of the force in an unofficial capacity. I don't have arrest powers. I am merely trying to find out if Emerson left Canada. We heard he had family down here. So, Sheriff Jefferson, can you help me?"

"The name don't mean nothing to me, but I'll have a look-see through my wanted posters and talk to a few people, and then I'll get back to you. Where'll you be?" he asked.

"Well, I'm headed over to the saloon … meeting my friend. I suppose we could wait there."

The sheriff nodded. "Might take a while."

"That's all right. We'll wait for you, Sheriff, and much obliged."

With that the Mountie turned to leave, snapping his finger and saying: "Come on, Red, time to go."

CHAPTER EIGHTEEN

Lucas saw White Bear standing outside the saloon. The Lakota was looking down the street nervously.

"You must be as thirsty as I am," Donovan said when he arrived at the saloon. "Come on, let's go inside."

White Bear hesitated, but with a little more coaxing, he followed the Mountie through the doors and into the saloon. As usual Red followed, but Lucas gave him the command to stay in the corner near the door. The malamute whimpered his displeasure, but otherwise complied with his master's order.

The two men approached the bar where a short fat bartender, wearing a stained shirt and a string tie, looked at White Bear with obvious contempt.

"Two beers, please," Lucas ordered.

"We don't serve no redskins here," the barman snapped, wiping the bar counter down with a dirty rag, never taking his eye off White Bear.

Donovan exhaled loudly and shrugged his shoulders, then he leaned over the bar and grabbed the barkeep's arm just above the elbow in a clawlike grip and slowly squeezed. The Donovans were known for their strength, but Lucas had also learned about pressure points from one of the hand-to-hand fighting instructors in the Mounties. The pain caused by such a pinching grab was considerable, even though it would hardly be obvious to the other patrons of the saloon.

"You won't have to," Donovan said quietly while continuing to clamp down on his arm. "I'm the one ordering two beers, and what I do with them once I sit down over at that table is my own business. You got a problem with that?"

The barman grimaced and shook his head. "No ... no, sir, none at all. Two beers coming up."

Lucas released his grip and motioned for White Bear to take a seat at the table he had pointed to. Then he looked the bartender in the eye. "Oh, and in case you might be planning on reaching for that weapon stashed behind the bar, that wolf over there is trained to rip your throat out." He gestured at Red, sitting at attention by the door now, watching them.

The barman actually gulped and nodded. "Got it."

Lucas slapped a coin down, grabbed the beers, and took them over to the table. He returned to the bar and grabbed a couple of hard-boiled eggs that were in a bowl on the counter before taking a seat.

"Might as well have something to eat," Lucas said. "We might be here for a little while. The local sheriff is checking out things for me. He might have some information about the man I'm looking for."

White Bear just grunted and nodded. He was obviously uncomfortable with his surroundings. A look at the hard cases around the room told Lucas that White Bear was justified in his uneasiness. Donovan retrieved salt from a small dish situated on a table at the side of the bar and sprinkled it on his egg. He nodded his head at the other egg, indicating to White Bear that he should take it. The Sioux picked it up and held it out to Donovan, who sprinkled on the remaining granules cupped in his hand.

They waited at the table, ignoring the hostile glances they received from the occupants of the bar. As Donovan finished a second beer, two bulky trappers entered, not swinging but slamming the batwing doors apart. As the two scanned the room with brows furrowed, breathing loud enough for all to hear, Donovan couldn't help but notice that they spent a little too much time studying the table where he sat with White Bear.

He had noticed the look of recognition on both their faces as they looked at him.

"Trouble," he told White Bear under his breath.

"White men no want me here?" he asked.

Lucas shook his head. "No, I don't think that's it. They didn't even look at you. It's me they're locked on. Funny thing is, I don't have any idea who they are. Why would I, not being from around here?"

Donovan vigilantly watched the two trappers as they walked up to the bar and ordered shots of whiskey. Again, Lucas caught one of them glancing over his shoulder in his direction.

"Hate to ask you this, my friend, since I could use the back up, but I need you to leave the saloon," Donovan advised White Bear. "If they follow you, I'll be right behind them with Red, but, if they don't, then it's definitely me they're interested in. Of course, it might be my imagination, and we can both just leave. If nothing happens, we'll go see the sheriff on the way out of town."

"White Bear no afraid, but—"

"I get it," Lucas replied. "This is not your fight, and I don't expect you to become involved. I mean that."

The Indian nodded, rose, and cautiously left the saloon without another word.

Lucas sipped his beer and inched his chair back from the table. When, after a few moments, he realized that neither of the two men was going to make a move to follow White Bear, Lucas got up and went to the bar.

"I'll have another beer," he told the barkeep.

One of the two trappers turned to face him. "You the fella lookin' for Jack Emerson?" he asked.

Donovan was surprised by the question, but, because of it, he knew he had made a mistake in Elk Grove in talking to the sheriff, but he also knew he was on the right trail.

"Could be," Lucas replied.

"Well, we's Emersons, too, and we don't like no Canucks trackin' our kin."

"I'm sorry, but I'm a little confused," Lucas said to the man.

That was not the response the man had been expecting. He cocked his head. "Yeah, what's got you so confused?"

"Well, for one thing, when you say you don't like *Canucks*, do you mean all Canadians ... or just the ones interested in the killers in your family?" Lucas asked, then he winked at the man.

That was enough to trigger the response Donovan had been waiting for. The trapper closest to him, the one who had braced him, turned and growled: "Why you lousy son of a bitch!" He drew his arm back to throw a roundhouse punch, but before he could land it, Lucas tossed his beer into the trapper's face.

The other man started to reach for his sidearm, when Lucas yelled out: "Red, gun arm!"

Before the trapper's gun had even cleared leather, Red struck. The big dog's bite, which wrenched the man's arm back, was more than sufficient to break his forearm, and the trapper fell to the ground, groaning in agony. This man was no longer a threat.

"Red, guard him," Donovan ordered just to keep the fight fair.

The large trapper, with a full beard and a scar running down his right cheek, was wiping the beer from his face. While his arms were raised, Lucas took advantage by elbowing him sideways, right in the solar plexus.

A big man with a hard gut might have taken a blow like that and stayed up, but when you aren't expecting it, the point of an elbow striking just below the end of the sternum will put you down for the count. The trapper never had a chance, and he crumbled to the ground, gasping for air.

Donovan unsnapped the flap on his holster and looked around the room. "Don't anyone move," he ordered.

The speed with which Donovan had taken down the two trappers, Emersons at that, convinced the occupants in the saloon that it wasn't worth trying to take on this powerhouse of a man. The presence of the growling malamute with a bite like a timber wolf further discouraged any interference with the tall Canadian.

Donovan turned around toward the barkeep. "Didn't get a chance to enjoy that last beer," he said, and the bartender quickly refilled his glass. The Mountie took his time drinking the beer as the two trappers slowly recovered.

When he finished the beer, he set down several coins on the bar before turning and lightly kicking the trapper with the beard.

"Time to take a walk," he said as he motioned with his gun for the two men to get up.

The two Emersons pushed themselves up off the floor very cautiously. "March," Donovan ordered as he escorted them through the bar and out the door, occasionally poking one or the other with his gun.

"The jail," the Mountie stated, as the two men hesitated outside the batwings, where White Bear stood to the left of the doorway. The dog growled at the trappers as the two reluctantly turned to the right, their shoes making scuffing sounds on the wooden walkway. Not wanting any more surprises from any of the others in the bar, Donovan ordered Red to stay with White Bear. Red let out a whine, keeping his eyes on his master as he walked the pair over to the jail.

"What about my arm?" the trapper complained as he cradled his injured arm close to his body.

Donovan didn't bother to answer. As he shoved the two men through the door and into the front room of the jail, he holstered his firearm. But he did not fasten the snap on his holster.

"What the hell?" the sheriff exclaimed as he jumped up from the desk chair.

"Little problem at the saloon," Lucas explained. "Need to lock these two up."

The lawman eyed the two Emersons and swallowed before nodding at Donovan. He grabbed a key ring off a hook behind his desk, led the men to the nearest cell, and locked them in. The Mountie couldn't help but notice the look the traders gave the sheriff as they passed by him.

"Care to tell me what this is all about?" the lawman asked once he was back at his desk.

Lucas sat down opposite the sheriff, who sat down apprehensively at his desk. "They came after me at the saloon. So I think it's you who actually has some explaining to do," Donovan said as he leaned forward in the chair.

"Is that so?" Jefferson said, as his right arm slowly drifted off the desk and down to his side, a gesture that did not go unnoticed by the Mountie.

"Yes, it is, Sheriff. Seems they are kin to Jack Emerson," Lucas stated. "Now, seeing that I haven't been in this town more than a few hours and the only person I talked to was you ... And the only person who knows I'm a Canadian Mountie looking for an outlaw by the name of Jack Emerson is you. Well, you can see why I'm back here in your jail."

The sheriff smiled as he shifted in the chair, but Donovan's Webley revolver was already up, its big barrel staring the sheriff right in the face.

"Pistol ... butt first ... right here on the desk," Lucas snapped as he tapped the top of the desk with the index finger of his left hand. It was as though Donovan could see the wheels turning inside of the lawman's brain, trying to find a way out of the situation. The sheriff had no choice but to obey, once he heard the Mountie cock the revolver.

Donovan eased back on the trigger but kept the gun aimed as Jefferson set his gun down on the desk. "Now you want to tell me why?" Lucas said.

"He's kin o' mine, too. Other side of the family. My mother was Jack's aunt," Sheriff Jefferson explained.

"So, that pair, in there"—he waved his gun in the direction of the cellblock before centering it right back at the lawman—"are your cousins, too," Lucas said.

"Yes," the sheriff replied. "Unfortunately, I expected more from them."

"You thought you wouldn't have to dirty your hands, keep the office of the sheriff nice and clean. Free from any suspicion, eh?" The Mountie shook his head in disgust. "Some lawman."

"Jack ain't wanted for anything around here," the lawman argued.

"That's because he's been up in Alberta. And, truthfully, I really don't give a damn!" Donovan shouted. "So tell me, Sheriff, just where is Jack Emerson now?"

"I ain't tellin' you nothin'."

"I am going to say this just once," the Mountie said angrily. "Jack Emerson killed my brother, and nothing is going to stop me from finding him."

The sheriff chuckled and stood up. "Yeah? So that's it. Good luck and adios then."

Donovan turned cold inside. He stood up and walked around the desk. He put a hand on the sheriff's shoulder, pushing him back down into the chair. As he watched fear wash over the lawman's face, he pressed the barrel of his Webley revolver into the man's forehead.

"If I was you, I'd stay real still, Jefferson," he advised as he shifted the barrel of the gun onto the lawman's knee, "otherwise, I can assure you, it won't be pleasant. Now you can have it either way you like, Sheriff. You can tell me what I want to know now, and keep your kneecap, or you don't talk. But, in that case, you'll have to get along with one knee and be using a wooden crutch for support for the rest of your life. It really depends on how tough you are and how much this kin of yours means to you. Besides, I figure if I can't get the information I'm looking for out of you, I suspect those two back in the cells will be more than willing to talk once they see what I've done to you." Lucas shook his head. "Then, of course, you'll have lost use of your knee for nothing. Either way, I am not leaving here without the information I seek."

Pellets of sweat were forming across the lawman's forehead. "You're bluffing, Donovan. You're a Mountie. You got rules … a code. If word got back to your headquarters about how you're pushing around the law down here—"

Donovan didn't let Jefferson finish. "Do you see me wearing a uniform? As you pointed out before, I haven't got any authority down here. I'm off duty down here in your Wild West. Seems my loyalty to my kin might be a bit stronger than yours." Donovan stared into the lawman's eyes, and Jefferson couldn't stand up under the steellike gaze of the Mountie, and he dropped his head. Donovan put the nose of the revolver under the sheriff's chin and forced him to raise his head back up. "Maybe I shouldn't even bother with your kneecap," he said, and he cocked his gun.

The sheriff tried to push back his chair as he cried out: "All right, all right! Don't shoot. I'll tell you anything you want to know."

"You already know what I want to know, so I'd start talking if I were you."

"Don't do it, Jeff!" called out one of the trappers from the back of the jail. "If you tell him, you'll have the wrath of the whole Emerson clan on your back."

The sheriff glanced toward the cellblock, with a look of helplessness on his face. Donovan could smell the fear emanating from his body.

"How do I know you won't kill me, anyway?" Jefferson asked, his tongue clicking in his desert-dry mouth.

"You don't," Donovan said, "but I don't negotiate. And I just changed my mind. Say goodbye to your knee, after all."

The revolver quickly shifted to the lawman's knee, and as it did, the sheriff cried out: "Three miles northwest of Bannack.

His family has an old mining camp there. That's where he'll be, I swear. I heard him talking to Jed back there"—he tipped his head toward the cells, never taking his eyes off Donovan—"when he came through town."

The Mountie pushed the gun barrel deeper into the man's knee, and said: "And why should I believe you?"

"Jack came through here a couple weeks ago and told Jed where he was heading. Said there might be someone following him, and he told me to take care of it. Said he was going to hole up for a while around Bannack, you know, seeing's how he knows the area so well."

Donovan eased off the revolver and pulled the man to his feet. "Back there," he ordered, and pushed the gun into the lawman's back as he shuffled toward the cells.

Donovan shoved him into the empty cell next to the one that housed the two trappers. He shot a look at the two as if daring them to say something, then he locked the cell door, holstered the Webley, got ready to leave, but not before deciding to keep the key ring to slow down any pursuit. Before he headed out the door, a thought occurred to him.

"Where's the telegraph office in town?" he shouted.

"We ain't got one yet," one of the trappers yelled out, laughter apparent in his voice. "Where the hell you think you is, Helena?"

Good, Lucas thought. That meant there was no way for anyone to get word to Bannack quickly or warn Jack Emerson before he arrived. Lucas hoped that White Bear knew the fastest route to Bannack. But Donovan couldn't worry about that now. If someone were to try to overtake him, he would deal with it out on the trail. Still, it never hurt to buy as much time as possible. It was then that Donovan had another idea.

He went back to the sheriff's desk and took out a Wanted sheet from one of the desk drawers and turned it over. He doubted that this ploy would buy him any time, but it amused him as he wrote:

SHERIFF'S OFFICE IS HEREBY QUARANTINED

DUE TO SUSPICION OF SMALLPOX.

PLEASE IGNORE ANY SHOUTING FROM

QUARANTINED PRISONERS IN CELLS UNDER

PENALTY OF CONTAGION.

Lucas smiled to himself as he tacked the notice to the inside of the jail's window for all to see, knowing that his brother would have enjoyed this joke even more than he did himself.

As he stepped outside, Red came running up, and he ruffled the fur on the dog's head. He waved to White Bear and they went to buy a few supplies. As the two mounted up to leave town, the Lakota turned and asked his companion: "Would you really shoot the lawman in knee, if he not talk?" In response to Lucas' quizzical look, White Bear explained: "Listen by window. Heard talk."

Donovan looked over at White Bear and shook his head. "I honestly don't know for sure, my friend."

Lucas whistled for Red, put a spur to his horse, and rode out without looking back.

The Lakota shrugged and mumbled to himself: "If was White Bear's brother, he shoot man."

CHAPTER NINETEEN

The Canadian and his guide rode for two more days before White Bear began acting strangely to Donovan's mind. He started asking the Mountie to ride out ahead while he would hang back on the trail for a couple of hours before he would catch up again. The practice continued into the third day. Each time, when he returned, he would look back, slow down, and rub the back of his neck.

Finally, the Indian stopped, and said to Donovan: "We are being followed."

The Mountie stopped to look back and study their back trail. "You think they're the men from Elk Grove? Emerson's kin?" Lucas asked.

"Don't know. Who else?" White Bear shrugged. "We must take care. Come."

White Bear and Lucas rode at a fast gallop for a while before the Lakota finally stopped at a narrow part of the trail.

"If want get to Bannack fast, men must come this way, otherwise lose many days.

Donovan surveyed their surroundings. This part of the trail was a ravine with steep slopes and a stand of trees on either side.

"What do you have in mind?" the Mountie asked.

"Block road. Hide. When men stop, we shoot dead from behind trees," White Bear suggested.

Lucas considered the plan for a moment before shaking his head. "We can't do that," he finally said.

"Why not?" White Bear asked.

"Well, for one thing we aren't positive it's Emerson's kin following us. For another, if it is them, they haven't done anything that gives us the right to shoot them down. After all, as much as I would like to see those two dead, they are trying to protect their own family. Same as me, really."

The Lakota grunted. "Emerson kill brother. Make sense kill these Emerson people, too."

"Maybe so, White Bear, maybe so, but this pony solider won't kill someone just because they were born with a certain family name. Even if it is a lousy one. That's why I put them in jail in the first place."

"What want do?" White Bear asked. He looked back down the trail again. "Not safe to have behind us. You want them go through to warn the man that kill your brother? Maybe Emerson man get away again."

Donovan nodded, but he was more interested in a runt-like tree toward the top of the slope he had been studying as White Bear spoke. He dismounted and walked down the trail to where it curved sharply to the left. He then remounted and rode back past White Bear. He stopped and turned his horse around to study the trail. "It just might work," he said aloud.

"What work? What we do?" the Lakota asked.

"Ever snare a rabbit?" Lucas asked.

The Indian nodded. "Bend branch. Catch with string."

The Mountie grinned. "That's right, my friend. But we'll use a rope." He pointed out the tree he thought they could use to their advantage.

"Here's what I have in mind," Donovan explained. "We set up a trap so that when the men ride through here, their horses' hoofs

will hit a trip rope we tie to that runty tree that we're going to use
by bending it over. Once the tied rope is tripped, the tree will then
straighten up and pull a second rope, right across the trail, here at
the narrowest part." Lucas pointed out the spot to his companion.
"They won't even see what hit them when the rope tightens across
the trail right about level with their neck. It should take them right
off their horses."

White Bear pointed to a different spot. "Why not put rope
there? Be easier."

The Mountie shook his head. "No, I don't think so. We can't
count on how fast they will be riding. They might spot the rope
and stop. What I have in mind is covering the tether with dirt and
debris, so they won't spot it. If we set it right, the second rope will
spring tight before they even have a chance to stop."

"Unless they are walking horses when come to curve," White
Bear pointed out.

"They're in a hurry to warn Emerson. They won't be walking
their horses, I'm sure of it," Lucas insisted.

"If riding fast, no need bend tree. Just stretch rope."

"The glass is always half empty, is it?" Donovan said.

"What glass?" White Bear asked, not sure what the Mountie
was asking him.

"Never mind. Let's just do it my way. Either way, it's a gamble."

"No work, then we kill?" the Lakota asked.

Donovan shook his head. "Let's cross that bridge when we
come to it."

White Bear looked down the trail, shook his head, even more
puzzled than a minute before. "No bridges here to Bannack," he said.

"Great. Makes it easier then," Donovan said, grinning. "Come
on, we've got work to do."

The two men worked together to bend the scrawny tree over.
They then tethered it down with a rope, which ran low along the
trail and had been wrapped around a notched piece of wood they

had driven firmly into the ground. A second rope reached from the bent tree over to a larger tree and then back across to a big tree limb located just around the curve.

When they were through, they rode their horses up the slope to a point that, while not visible from the gully, still gave them a good view of the trail below.

White Bear took his rifle from his scabbard and started to walk away.

"Where are you going?" Lucas asked.

"Ahead. If this no work, I kill them for you."

"I thought you didn't want to get involved?" Lucas asked.

"Not in town. Too many *white eyes*. No like—how you say?—odds there. But out here, I not worry. Brother of pony soldier now like brother of White Bear."

Donovan was deeply touched. "Thank you, my friend. But just wait and see if this works before you pull the trigger on that thing. All right?"

The Indian shrugged. "If you say. But White Bear think pony soldier always do things hard way."

Donovan grinned. "Oh, trust me. Not always."

It took two hours of waiting before the three men finally showed up. The Lakota had been right. It was the sheriff and the two trappers, the cousins of Jack Emerson.

"Quiet, boy," Lucas said to his dog, who began to whimper softly at the sight of the trio. "Easy, Red, just let them come on in."

The men were riding at a fast lope and hit the trip line just as Donovan had hoped. When the skinny tree straightened, it pulled the slack from the main rope, tugging it tight. The whole thing worked as if it had been rigged to a pulley, and before the men knew what had hit them, their shoulders collided with the rope line. All three men were catapulted backward, almost somer-saulting off their horses, and hitting the ground hard. The trapper with his arm in a sling let off with a flurry of oaths.

"That must have hurt," the Mountie said, laughing while patting his dog on the head and watching the trio's horses gallop off.

White Bear stayed hidden up on the slope with his rifle aimed at the three men as Donovan made his way down onto the trail. When he reached the bottom of the slope, his pistol was out and trained on the riders, and he ordered them to drop their holsters. The man with the injured arm fumbled awkwardly for a moment, but finally got it off.

"Got out of jail faster than I expected, Sheriff," Donovan addressed Jefferson.

"No thanks to you. We was lucky the town doc came by and saw the sign. He knew it was a lie. Him being the only one allowed to quarantine someone in that kind of situation."

The Mountie laughed again. "I'll bet it still took some explaining," he said, as he glanced at the trapper with his arm in a sling. "The doc showing up worked out well for you, I see," he said to the man.

"All because of you and your damned mutt," the man grumbled.

"What are you going to do with us now?" the trapper asked angrily.

"I should kill you, so you can't stop me from finding Jack Emerson," Donovan replied.

The sheriff shook his head. "You're a Mountie. Your office won't allow it."

"Oh, I'd dare all right. But, at least for now, I won't." He used his Webley pistol to point with. "Stand together over there. *Move!*" he ordered, his distaste for these men growing.

Donovan intended they have their backs to him, so he could safely search them for other weapons, but before he could herd them all together, the sheriff spun around and pulled out a hidden pocket pistol from under his coat.

A shot rang out and the sheriff was pitched backward. White Bear had fired from his cover. Almost simultaneously, however, the man with the sling turned and rammed into Lucas with his shoulder, which made him curse loudly upon impact.

Donovan was thrown sideways by the rush, and his pistol was

knocked from his grip. Emerson's cousin watched the gun slide and there was no doubt that he intended to dive for it, despite his bad arm. Turns out, attacking Lucas Donovan was the last mistake he would ever make. The big malamute jumped into action, and the man went down with Red's teeth clamped down on his throat. He wasn't even able to scream, as the dog's teeth punctured his neck in several places.

With a desperate look on his face, the remaining trapper pulled a knife from his right boot. Lucas knew that trying to recover his pistol at that distance would be futile. Charlie Two Knives had taught the Donovan boys well. *When going up, unarmed, against a man with a knife, expect to get cut. You must accept that and forget your fear. Keep your distance until your attacker commits. For all his fancy moves, he cannot cut you until you are inside a circle that represents the length of his arm plus the blade. If you are forced to back up, it is more likely you will stumble and fall, and that will be fatal. So, never fight in a straight line. Always circle. Remember, it is the blade that cuts or kills, but it is the hand that holds the knife. Since you can't attack cold steel, you must try to attack the hand and the arm that holds it.*

Lucas would try to defang the snake, as Charlie had called it.

The trapper lunged with his dagger, and Lucas pivoted back with his right foot. He was now sideways to the thrusting attack, so that he was facing the outer side of the trapper's arm.

Still more of Charlie's words about knife fights came back to Donovan. *Stun the mind and the body collapses. Take the attacker's mind off his plan and make him refocus on his own pain. Remember, there are certain points on the body where a blow will cause such discomfort that the brain will forget everything else, even if only for a moment, and in a knife fight, a moment is a lifetime. The eyeball is such a point, as is the front of the throat where the windpipe is.*

Some years ago, he had bashed his shin into a bed frame one night, and the pain was excruciating. His recollection of hopping around his dark bedroom reminded him that the shin was one of these points of pain.

This time, as the trapper's thrusting arm passed uncomfortably close to Donovan's chest, the Mountie deflected the knife arm away, using his left hand, while simultaneously using a sideways savate kick to the front midpoint of the man's right shin.

The shock and pain caused by the Mountie's boot hitting the attacker's shin was so great that it temporarily relaxed the muscles in the man's knife arm, thus allowing Lucas to use his right hand to grab and twist the man's wrist. He pushed out on his opponent's elbow with his left hand, while with his right he bent the man's wrist inward, directing the knife back toward the attacker's own chest. He was dead before his body hit the ground—from the bullet the Lakota had fired.

As Donovan stool there, looking at the three men, White Bear descended from the slope.

"Men all dead," White Bear said.

"Yes. They are," Lucas said, shaking his head. He walked over to his pack horse and retrieved the ax. "And now I have to bury them."

"Why not leave here? Animals take away."

"I can't do that," Lucas explained. "It's not my way."

"Pony soldier not want to kill men like White Bear say, but now all dead anyway," the Lakota remarked.

"Well, I tried," Lucas replied, looking up at his companion. "So, what's your point?"

"White Bear still think pony soldier do things hard way."

Donovan headed off the trail with the ax, hoping to keep the graves out of the sight of passersby. He jabbed the ax into the hard ground, pushing down on it to drive it deeper. As he labored, he couldn't help thinking: *Maybe you are right, my Lakota friend. Maybe you are right after all.*

CHAPTER TWENTY

Two days later, the Mountie and his guide arrived at the outskirts of the town of Bannack. Lucas was growing comfortable around White Bear, as was Red, in spite of the Sioux's reticent personality.

"You saved my life back there, you know," Lucas said, the town coming into view.

White Bear merely shrugged. "No have choice. Took money to get you here. Like you say ... was contract. You no live, you no make it here, then White Bear no deserve money."

Donovan laughed. "That's one way of looking at it, I suppose. Well, rest easy, my friend. You are an honest man and you clearly earned your pay."

They had found the horses of the two trappers and the sheriff on the trail and had tied one to each of their three horses. Outside Bannack, Lucas untied the lead rope attached to the brass ring on his saddle and the one attached to the pack horse and handed them to White Bear.

"Take the three extra horses and all that comes with them, White Bear. You earned it all."

The Lakota looked surprised. "You no keep?"

"Nope. I won't be needing them." Lucas nodded his head back in the direction of the trail. "And those three back there on the trail certainly won't be needing them, either."

White Bear stuck out his hand and clasped Donovan's forearm firmly.

"Pony soldier good man. White Bear remember always."

"And I, you. Sure you won't change your mind and come into town with me? Might get us a good meal and some cold beer."

White Bear shook his head. "Think best to get the horses out of this area. White Bear move on now. Beer taste good, but remember, pony soldier, what happen in bar in Elk Grove."

"I guess you're right, White Bear. In fact, you might not want to go back the way we came. Someone might recognize the horses and ask a few too many questions."

White Bear shook his head and looked around. "Go north, look for my people. Maybe go up to your country."

"If you ever do, be sure to look me up at Fort Macleod. I owe you much, my friend." White Bear took hold of the lead ropes of the horses and turned his mount. "May the Great Spirit be with you always, Donovan," he said as he glanced back one last time before riding off.

The Mountie breathed deeply. He would miss White Bear, but as he expelled his breath, it was what lay ahead that was on his mind. He looked back to catch a fleeting glimpse of the Lakota.

* * * * *

As he rode into Bannack, Donovan straightened in his saddle. A shiver, like a warning, traveled up his spine. That Jack Emerson had warned his relatives to be on the lookout for someone following him convinced Donovan the outlaw would have more people helping him in his home town.

Lucas was well aware that his skills at reading sign would never be as good as that of his brother or of White Bear. If he had any advantage, it was Red who was always alert to trouble. So far on this journey, the dog had saved him more times than he could count; a few times his presence alone had made the difference.

The sound of ringing hammers penetrated deep into Donovan's ears as he moved through the town that was clearly drawing in new settlers and businesses. Still, it had many of the signs of a primitive frontier mining town. Stores set up in large open-front tents stood right alongside new wood-framed ones. Large freight wagons made their way down the dirt streets, and men with various tools shuffled down the plank walkways, which were being extended to the entrances of the new construction.

Donovan made his way down the dirt street to its far end, where a large stable and a corral were located. A sign made from an old battered piece of wood painted white read: POP RYAN, LIVERYMAN.

Here, Lucas dismounted and extended his hand to an aging bald man, standing outside. The man scratched his head as he assessed the Mountie.

"Take it you're Pop," said Donovan. "Got room to put up my horses for a few days?" he asked.

"No problem," replied the older man as he shifted his porkpie hat. "It'll be fifty cents a day, full or part time, but that includes grain. Ain't no box stalls yet, just standin' stalls, but they's kept real clean, mister."

Donovan's quick but observant glance around revealed the man's pride was justified. There weren't too many flies buzzing around, which was uncommon for a stable, and the manure pile was kept a decent distance from the stalls. There were large clean bins for the grain, and the hay appeared fresh, with no evidence of mold. The nails had been countersunk during construction, so there were none sticking out to cut the horses.

"Sounds fair to me," Lucas said, nodding his approval. "Can you recommend a place to stay around here? Maybe some place I can clean up?"

"Head down that ways a bit. A good hotel's right around the corner." He pointed back the way Lucas had come. "They got real clean rooms. They's a barbershop next door where you can shave and take a bath. Cost you a buck." The liveryman removed his hat again and wiped his head with a kerchief he pulled from his pocket. "Funny. Horses is bigger and take longer to bathe, but men cost more fer some reason."

"Thanks for your help." Lucas pulled his saddle bags and bedroll from the pack horse.

"Say, that's one of them Canadian trooper saddles, ain't it?" Pop Ryan asked, noticing the split seat and the cross bars underneath.

"Sure is," Lucas replied.

"They look like real ballbusters ... kinda like McClellans. I rode one once a while back. Turned out to be real comfortable once you got used to it. They ride a little higher than the other saddles, but you don't notice it much."

Donovan nodded. "That's been my experience."

Pop took a good look at the young man. He took note of his posture and the campaign hat he wore. "You're a Mountie," he said, and it wasn't a question.

After a moment's hesitation, Lucas answered: "Not on duty now. I'm just visiting."

Pop Ryan looked around the dirty town and grinned.

"Visiting? Bannack? Sure you are," the liveryman commented, and shrugged. "Whatever you say ... ain't no business o' mine."

"Just take good care of my horses. Especially Handsome Harry here, and we'll be friends."

Pop looked at the horse's mule ears. "Handsome, huh? You know, somehow that fits," he said, and chuckled to himself. "Don't you worry, I'll take real good care of them."

"See you later," Lucas said, tipping his hat at the old man before throwing his bags over his shoulder and starting down toward the hotel. The big red-and-white malamute trotting alongside as always.

The hotel was called the Lucky Strike. It was a two-story affair with new windows at either side of the front entry to the building. Lucas noted that a third floor was under construction with big crossbeams still being hammered into place.

He entered and approached the front desk. The lobby was clean but relatively plain. A thin man was at the desk, writing in the hotel's ledger. He had slick hair that was parted in the middle and he wore a small pair of spectacles. He looked up and smiled at Lucas.

"Afternoon, sir, how may I be of service?" he asked politely as he removed his glasses.

"I'd like a room for a few nights. Maybe a little longer. You are open, I assume?"

"Yes, sir, we are. The construction you probably noticed is a third floor addition. We'll be the tallest building when it's done."

"Business must be good," Lucas commented.

"Well, the town is growing, and we hope to continue to do so right along with it," the clerk stated proudly.

Donovan nodded his head down toward his dog. "Any problem with him staying with me? He's no trouble."

The man leaned over the desk and smiled. "Good-looking animal. Malamute, isn't he?"

"That's right. Purebred."

"I'm a collie man myself. Grew up with one. Great breed, if you don't mind cleaning your house with a rake."

Lucas laughed. "They do shed a mite."

"Putting it mildly, sir," the clerk replied. "But never a more caring or heroic breed, iffen you ask me."

"Well, I could argue that with you, but not all folks like the same breed of dog. So I take it you're saying it's all right if Red stays with me?"

The clerk nodded. "No problem for me. Besides, my family owns the place. They're all dog folks, too, so it'll be fine. You want my opinion, dogs are a better class of guest than a lot of the humans we've had over the years."

Lucas nodded his head, chuckling at the remark. "I can assure you, Red, here, will behave himself. Been told there's a barbershop close by I can get a shave … maybe take a bath?"

"We hope to get our own bathhouse set up in time … it'd be convenient for our guests," the clerk explained. "For now, the place next store will have to suffice."

"Close enough for government work," Lucas joked. "I'm not that particular."

"It's a clean place, I assure you. Just mention that we sent you and they'll take two bits off the bill. Professional courtesy, so to speak."

"Thanks, I'll do that," Lucas replied. After signing the ledger, he picked up his things and was handed a key.

"Room two-oh-one. Second floor, on the left," the clerk explained, pointing to the nearby staircase. "If you need anything, just ask for me. The name's Shad."

"I appreciate it, Shad, and thanks." Lucas started toward the staircase with Red following, his furry tail happily wagging, knowing he might get a steak to eat.

After stowing his pack in the room, Lucas decided to check out the barbershop and get cleaned up before checking out the town. He briefly considered bringing the big Sharps rifle along, but decided it was unlikely he'd need it in town. He propped it in the corner behind the door and motioned to Red to follow him out.

Once on the street, Lucas smiled when he saw a couple of young boys playing hoops and sticks. It had been the most popular game played at school back in Alberta. His teacher had said the game had been around for thousands of years. He remembered hitting a stick against a two-foot-high hoop, trying to keep it turning as he ran beside it.

Thinking of that reminded him of Jamie's favorite game, cabin fever ring toss, as they called it. Jamie had the hand-eye coordination needed to swing the two-inch ring hanging from a string attached to the ceiling and hook it to a nail hammered halfway into the wall. Jamie would play the ring toss game for hours, whereas Lucas found it frustrating because it was harder than it looked. Funny, Lucas thought, that remembering his brother at play made him feel both happy and sad at the same time.

The barbershop was easily identified by the pole—painted red, blue, and white—hanging beside the entrance.

Back at Fort Macleod, the Mountie always enjoyed the long conversations he had with the fort's barber, Max Friedman, who loved to tell stories and expound on almost any subject. It was from him that Donovan learned that, in the past, barbers had done a lot more than groom men's hair, including practicing dentistry, bloodletting, fortune-telling, and phrenology, which involved reading the bumps on a person's head. He and Jamie would pretend to read the men's head while in the barracks at night as entertainment.

The barber's pole in Bannack had a brass ball at its top, which Friedman said was where barbers kept their leeches for the bloodletting. Also, according to him, the red and white of the pole symbolized the clean and bloodstained bandages of the procedure. Recalling all the odd bits of history Friedman had told him, he wondered if the addition of the blue stripe was an American thing. Lucas considered the barber's pole to be a clever way for an occupation to draw attention to itself.

Lucas walked inside and was immediately met by the strong scent of bay rum and alcohol. The two barber chairs on the right were occupied. The barber was just finishing up with a fellow, and the other was occupied by a man lounging back and reading a

Beadle dime novel. Two men sat on chairs to the left. Both were nodding off.

A short, thin man with a handlebar mustache addressed Donovan as he brushed hairs off his customer's collar. "Welcome, stranger. What'll it be … shave and a haircut?"

It had been weeks since Lucas had taken the time to properly groom himself, so he decided to go for the works, even though he could shave himself. As he shrugged out of his jacket, he answered in the affirmative, adding: "Was told by Shad over at the hotel, I could get a bath here, too. And at discount."

The man nodded. "Shad was right on all counts. Best bathtubs west of Helena, matter of fact."

Donovan still held the door ajar so that Red wouldn't start scratching at it. "Mind if I down my dog inside?" he asked the barber. "Won't bother anyone."

The barber leaned over to get a better view of Red. His eyes widened, but he thought the stranger looked reliable. "Sure, I guess so. As long as he don't make a mess. The tubs are right back there … behind the curtain." He indicated a doorway with a thick velvety-looking curtain drawn over it. "Six bits for twenty minutes," he told Donovan.

"Six bits, huh? The water hot?"

"Is the water hot?" the barber repeated, as he shook his head and laughed. "There's a hot spring near here. I pay a young lad to fill and tend to the baths all day long. He can make you boil like a lobster, if you so desire. Keeps the tubs real clean, too. A gratuity for the boy is always appreciated, if you're pleased."

"Warm will be just fine. Mind if I bathe before that shave and haircut, or might there be a wait?"

"That'll work out just fine." The barber pointed to the chairs where the two groggy men were sitting. "Leroy, there"—the barber pointed to the fellow on the left, who opened his eyes briefly at his name being mentioned—"just needs a trim. Charlton, the one on the right, just hangs around all day and sleeps. Think he's just trying to hide from his old lady."

Charlton opened his eyes. "Tain't at all so," he said. "I'm just giving her a break from my company, so she don't get bored with me. Making her 'preciate and miss me, so to speak. Like that saying ... absence makes the heart grow fonder."

The fellow in the barber chair, reading the novel looked up to say: "Absinthe?"

"Absinthe what?" LeRoy asked.

"Makes the heart grow fonder."

"Absence," LeRoy said, and spelled out the word. He paused, then turned to Charlton and asked: "What you want to bet she don't even notice you're gone?"

Lucas had to bite his tongue to keep from laughing, but the barber broke out into loud guffaws. When he finally got his breath back, he wiped the tears from his eyes.

At the pause in the banter, Lucas asked: "You want your money up front?"

The barber shook his head. "When you're done is fine. Don't rightly think you'll take off without your clothes, and, besides, who'd want to steal a bathtub, anyway?"

"A low down *dirty* crook, eh?" Lucas quipped.

"Good one," the barber commented, grinning largely. "I'll have to remember that." Then he motioned to the curtain again. "Go on back. The boy's name is Toby. Mine's Edwin."

"Nice to meet you, Edwin," Lucas said, and headed to the back room. "Red, there in the corner. Down," he told the malamute. "If he starts moving around, Edwin, just let me know. As long as he can hear me, he should stay put."

It was obvious Edwin was impressed with how obedient the dog appeared to be as he circled before lying down. "Good enough," said the barber. "By the time you finish with your bath, I should be ready for you. Leroy's getting a little thin on top ..."

"Hey, watch what you're saying, Edwin!"

"Sorry," the barber said, chuckling. "I thought it was obvious."

Donovan pulled the curtain aside and ducked as he walked into a surprisingly large room. There were four tubs, each sectioned off by privacy curtains. The tubs were ceramic, set in a wooden frame. In the middle of the room stood a boy about twelve years of age.

"You must be Toby," Lucas said.

"Yes, sir, I am. The next bath ready will be that one over on the right. We have soap and towels, but if you want scents, that will be a little extra. You know, like perfume ... but for men."

Lucas began removing his shirt, boots, and pants. "No thanks, soap will do just fine."

"Yes, sir. I just added more hot water to that there tub, but I can fetch more if you want it even hotter."

Lucas tested the tub with his hand. "This will do, and you don't have to *sir* me, Toby, I work for a living. Name's Lucas."

The boy smiled and pulled a couple of towels off a shelf. "Yes, sir. But I'm gonna get some more water, anyway. It tends to cool off pretty quick, and with the hot spring so close, it ain't really no problem."

From the eagerness of his service, it was obvious Toby was working for tips. And Lucas figured the boy would probably end up earning more than just a good living, no matter what he did.

"Just go on and get in," Toby said as he walked over to a wall where a large hourglass hung on a rotating bracket. He turned it over. "Just keep an eye on the sand. If it runs out, I have to charge you extra."

"Thanks, I'll remember that, Toby." As Donovan eased himself into the tub, it felt so good to his sore body that he gave serious consideration to ignoring the hourglass altogether. But a half hour later, after tipping Toby for his attention, Donovan emerged from the back room, clean and refreshed.

Edwin was waiting for him behind one of the two empty

chairs, which he swiveled as Donovan entered the shop. "Please take a seat, mister."

"I'll just sit back and relax while you dandify me," the Mountie said, stepping into the chair.

"What's your pleasure?" the barber asked, draping a large white sheet right below his neck that extended all the way down to his knees.

"Shave and a light trim. Make sure you clean up the back. Also, I'd appreciate the loan of a bowl, so I can give Red some water." Edwin was quick to oblige, telling Donovan to stay where he was, that he'd take care of it. As Edwin got a bowl of water from the back room, Lucas unsnapped the flap on his holster out of habit. Most of the Mounties carried their holsters cross-draw style on the left side of the waist, since most seemed to be right-handed, which made for a slower draw than when worn on one's dominant side. Besides, the cross-draw works better when seated in a tight space. Lucas wasn't expecting trouble yet, but if something came up, he didn't want to be hemmed in by the arms of the barber chair. Also, since crossing the border, he felt more strongly that it paid to be cautious in this country.

After the barber started soaping up his shaving brush, he attempted to make small talk, asking Donovan: "Haven't seen you before. Just get into town?"

"Yep. I just rode in," Lucas replied, keeping his answers short.

"Planning on staying a while?" Edwin pursued. Although it was custom in the West not to pry too closely into another man's affairs, the barber seemed to be an exception to the rule.

"Not trying to be nosy, mind you," Edwin added, "it's just that we can always use new clients." He lathered up Lucas' face with the foamy shaving brush.

The Mountie chuckled. "Let's see how this turns out, before I make any long-term commitments, Edwin."

The barber nodded in agreement, sharpening his pearl-handled straight razor on the leather strop that hung on the chair. Edwin began shaving Donovan's chin. He stopped asking questions, since his client couldn't respond easily under the circumstances, but he did complain about the noise that had taken over the town since expansion had begun.

As Edwin wiped the razor on his apron, the Mountie said: "I plan on checking the area out for possible mining prospects. Maybe buy some land or a house."

"Well, you came to the right place. Bannack is known for mining. We still got a lot of ore to pull out of the ground, but, of course, things at the mines aren't as plentiful as when they first started digging around here. It was called Grasshopper Creek back then, 'cause of all the insects."

"Well, the town seems to be prospering now," Lucas observed.

"Gettin' right sizable lately, that's for sure," the barber agreed.

"Well, last time I came through, I met a couple of men in a saloon who suggested I might look north or maybe northwest of town for a place that might be up for sale. They said there was a family had some good ground they might be interested in selling. Name was Anderson … no, that wasn't it. Em …Emmett? Emerson, that was it. Heard of them?"

At the name Emerson, Donovan felt a stiffening in the barber's body, and his hand seemed a bit unsteady.

"Whoa there, old chap," Lucas said, bringing his hand out from under the sheet and trying to steady the barber's arm. "Just want a shave. Something wrong?"

Edwin thought a moment before replying. "You heard anything else about the Emersons?"

Lucas shook his head. "Like I said … only that they had a mine they weren't working and might be interested in selling. Why? Was I steered wrong?"

Edwin wiped his forehead with the sleeve of his shirt. He looked around before answering. "Well, I don't like speaking ill of

anyone, and please keep this to yourself, but Jack Emerson is …
well, frankly he's an owl hoot. He was gone for a number of years,
but I heard he's back."

In his line of work, Donovan had heard the Western expression
more than once—*owl hoot trail*. He took the meaning to be an
outlaw skirting the law, which was what Emerson was doing.

"That bad, huh?" Donovan commiserated.

Edwin leaned in closer. "As bad as they come," he whispered.
"They say when he was a teenager, he used to torture animals. You
know the type … just bad through and through. Rumor is, that
up north across the border, Jack once shot a man in a hotel right
through the wall simply because the man's snoring bothered him.
Take my advice and stay clear of him. And his whole family."

"Well, I'll be careful, based on what you just told me, but I'm
sure if there's any trouble, the local sheriff would take care of it."

The barber shook his head. "See, that's the problem. We ain't
got none. The town's sheriff is missing. Rode out of town 'bout
three weeks back and nobody's seen him since."

"Nobody knows what happened?" Lucas asked.

"Nobody," the barber affirmed. "Said he'd be back by the end of
the day, 'cording to Pop, the liveryman. But he didn't come back at
all. It's like he just disappeared off the face of the earth."

"What about a deputy sheriff?" Donovan pursued.

"Nope. Ain't had one of those since the last one we had broke
his leg over a year ago. Since then no one's come forward to ask for
the job and nobody's willing to take it when it's offered to them,
neither," Edwin explained.

This information, Donovan knew, could turn out either to be
good or bad for him. On the one hand, he had no local authority to
turn to for back up, but, on the other, he wouldn't be butting heads
with the local lawmen. It appeared there was no one in Bannack to
stand in his way.

Lucas looked at himself in the barber's mirror when Edwin was finished. He nodded. "Nice job, Edwin. I appreciate it." He paid him and slapped his leg to arouse Red.

"Remember what I told you," Edwin warned. "Stay away from that place."

"Thanks again for the haircut … and the advice," Lucas said as he exited the barbershop, the big malamute by his side.

CHAPTER TWENTY-ONE

Donovan felt that Jack Emerson was now within his grasp, but he knew he would have to prepare for their next encounter. After considering his options, Lucas decided to scout around the Emerson property in the morning, even though he'd be less likely seen in the dark. Experience had taught him that such a rash move would give Emerson far too great an advantage, especially since Emerson was on his home ground and he knew the land like the back of his hand. Still, this murderer was much too dangerous to take without Donovan's having any knowledge of the man's hideout and its environs.

Every night before he went to sleep the last several weeks, the Mountie had done nothing but think about how he would behave and what he would do once they met. There would be none of the usual "give yourself up, and I'll assure you a fair trial" protocol. This man had murdered Jamie in cold blood without so much as a second thought. As far as Lucas Donovan was concerned this bushwhacker deserved nothing less than death.

He decided if he ran into his prey tomorrow morning, then he'd do what he had to do, and so much the better. But first, the Mountie's desire tended more toward the mundane: eliminating the growling coming from the pit of his stomach.

Donovan and Red studied the town, searching for a suitable café. They passed two places that served food, but Donovan could tell neither would allow Red to enter with him. Lucas noticed people sitting at tables inside a tent, the front of which was open. As the breeze picked up, Lucas caught the aroma of a stew, smelling rich and savory.

"I think we found dinner, Red," he said. A sign was nailed at a crooked angle to the tent frame.

TODAY'S SPECIAL IS THE SAME AS ALL OTHER DAYS.

BOWL OF BEEF STEW OR BOWL OF CHILI CON CARNE 50¢

CORN BREAD 5¢

BEER $1

TAKE IT OR LEAVE

When he approached the tent, several of the miners stopped eating to glance down at Red. One even whistled in admiration.

"Anyone mind if the dog stays with me while I eat?" Lucas asked politely.

Most of the men merely shook their heads, and one remarked it was a free country.

Donovan sat at the end of the far table while Red curled up on the ground beside him. A burly man with muttonchop sideburns, covered neck to ankles in a food-spattered white apron, approached them.

"You saw the sign. What'll it be?" he rasped.

"Two bowls of beef stew and one chili, and some cornbread," Lucas told him.

The man looked at him curiously. "Not tryin' to cut back on my own business, but that seems like a lot to eat, even for a gent your size. These is healthy sized bowls they is, and I'm proud to say it."

Lucas smiled and shook his head. "It smells so good, I wish I could have a bowl of each. But that would probably be a mistake, knowing how much my stomach must've shrunk over the last couple of weeks. No, the two stews are for my dog, here. Just the chili and the cornbread for me."

The man looked down at the malamute. "Judging by his size, maybe two bowls won't be enough?"

"It's a good place to start," Lucas said.

The man nodded. "As long as he sticks to the stew and don't eat any of my customers, we're fine. Anything to drink?"

Lucas nodded. "A beer for me and, if you don't mind, a bowl of water for Red here."

"Coming up," the man said, and went to get the food.

When the food was served, Lucas was glad he had chosen this place. The food was simple and flavorful. Red scarfed the food up in a matter of minutes. Donovan complimented the owner on the food.

Picking up dishes on the other end of the long table, the man thanked him, and added: "Lived for a while in Texas and worked the chuck wagon on a drive or two. Down there, there are three things necessary to being a good cook."

Lucas interrupted him. "Let me guess ... the coffee, stew, and chili."

The man laughed. "Got to be able to stand a spoon straight up in all three. Down in Texas, the chili don't always have beans in it, but I find it adds a little bulk and some zest to the mix."

"Tasted good to me." Lucas looked down as Red began licking the empty bowls again. "The stew was agreeable to my dog, which is pretty obvious."

"Mighty big animal you got there," the man said. "Could put you in the poorhouse trying to keep a dog like that in victuals."

"Maybe so, but he's the best sled dog north of the border," Lucas bragged. "He's pulled me out of many a tough fix." Donovan flashed to an image of Red helping him pull Jamie's body back up that gully.

"Something wrong, mister?" the man asked.

Lucas looked up into the man's face, realized he had been lost in his thoughts, which wasn't a good thing. "No, nothing ... I'm fine. My mind just wandered off, is all." He pulled coins from his pocket, telling the man to keep the change and motioned for Red to follow as he headed back to the hotel.

The man stood there for a moment, his hands on his hips, watching the pair leave. He shrugged his shoulders as another customer arrived in the tent.

CHAPTER TWENTY-TWO

Donovan was up early. He had gone to the hotel's kitchen the night before to inquire whether they could save any table scraps and leftovers and have them sent up in the morning for his dog. What arrived soon after he was up was more than ample for the dog and included beef and fish as well as a few vegetables. Lucas wasn't that hungry, but he knew he would need to eat something since he didn't know how long his scouting trip would take, so he ordered a couple of eggs and coffee.

Before leaving the room, Lucas adjusted the money belt, strapped on his holster, and checked the Webley revolver he carried. Although the gun had never left his side, he followed one of several gun rules that had been set down to him and Jamie when they were young and just beginning to handle weapons. *Always check a pistol and its rounds before carrying it. Every time. No matter what.*

Next, he collected the Sharps big-bore rifle and gave one last look around the room. Satisfied, he motioned for Red, then headed over to the livery stable.

Once he had saddled Handsome Harry, Lucas rode out in a northwesterly direction.

It had been a fitful night for him, tossing and turning as he relived the time he and Jamie had been tasked with putting an end to the crooked operator of a trading post.

Hunters and trappers complained that the trader was short-changing them on the goods they were bringing in to sell, using hollowed-out scales, but nobody could catch him in the act. It was Jamie's idea to catch him by taking in twenty pounds of beaver skins and seeing what weight the trader came up with.

As suspected, what Lucas brought in weighed almost four pounds less than it should have on the trader's scale. When Lucas revealed himself to be a Mountie, the trading post operator pushed him backward and grabbed for a hidden gun. He reacted so quickly, Lucas was taken completely off guard.

In the meantime, knowing no plan is foolproof, Jamie had quietly entered the post through the back door, even though he was supposed to stay with the sleds. He crept to the interior door leading to the storefront, which was partially ajar. He was able to see what was going on with the trader. He could see the sawed-off shotgun propped up against the counter behind the weighing station. He reacted almost at the same time the trapper did. Lucas fell backward, when the trader had grabbed for the shotgun, but, before he could raise it, Jamie literally dove over the counter from behind and tackled the man. The shotgun discharged both barrels with a loud roar. Fortunately, the blast was directed up and away, and by the time the trader threw off Jamie and untangled himself, he found a Webley revolver pointed directly at his face.

"I'm Constable Lucas Donovan, and I hereby arrest you for larceny, aggravated assault, and intent to kill a North-West Mounted Policeman."

The man looked up and spit: "Hell, he assaulted me!" He pointed at Jamie.

"He may not follow instructions very well," Lucas said, glancing up and giving his brother a quick grin, "but he's a Mountie, too. And since you fought with him, let's make that two counts of attacking a North-West Mounted Police."

While Jamie was handcuffing the trader, he told Lucas: "I may not follow instructions very well, Brother, but it's a good thing for you I didn't follow them this time."

It was the second time Jamie had saved him from certain death.

He couldn't get the thought out of his mind that he had let Jamie down when he didn't protect him from Emerson. That emptiness, that feeling, fueled his anger as he rode cautiously toward the Emerson property this morning.

He had been riding for over an hour, when he slowed his horse. He had a fairly good idea of the location of the Emerson family mine since he had visited the land office and had a good look at the maps of the area. Lucas had a plan in mind, but he knew that making a plan, and actually putting the plan into action, can be two entirely different things.

Once he knew he was closing in on the Emerson property, Lucas drew out the Sharps rifle. He proceeded slowly at a walk, constantly on the lookout for sign of an ambush. The malamute followed closely and quietly as he had been trained to do. After all their years together, the dog instinctively knew when they were on a hunt.

* * * * *

Jack Emerson had returned to the Emerson family's property, but he wasn't sitting back or relaxing. He was worked up and pacing like a caged animal. He detested the idea of working for a living, but he knew that soon he would have to leave the area in order to feed his cravings, which could only be satisfied by feeding off the terror of others. But more concerning at the moment was his sense that someone from across the border was after him. He could feel it. He couldn't kill with someone on his trail. The only way out of this for him was to get together a small bankroll and get away from the north country, maybe head for Colorado.

The family's mine had been abandoned some years previously, but Emerson's father had left a vein deep in the mine, untouched, in case of emergencies, and he had told Jack about it. Even if the vein didn't yield much, Emerson thought it might be enough for him to move on to better hunting grounds.

Emerson had always considered himself a cautious man, and he believed that if anyone did come looking for him, they would have to do so by day. The forested area around the place, once the sun set, was extremely dense and dark. There was only one small trail that led to the mine and the cabin, which twisted and turned so much that it would be nearly impossible to follow without light. Hell, even someone familiar with the trail would have a hard time following it through that dense brush without a torch or an oil lamp, which would be a dead giveaway to anyone in the cabin that someone was approaching.

That was why Emerson only worked the vein at night, and only for short periods, not turning on his lamp until he was shielded deep inside the mine.

By day, Emerson hid out in the dilapidated shack that had served as the family home for so many years. It was old and mouse-infested, but it did have two advantages. First, it had a roof that didn't leak, and secondly, it had windows in all four sides so that no one could sneak up on him.

He was currently seated on a wooden stool outside the front door of the split log shack, in the process of skinning a couple of rabbits and a squirrel he had snared earlier that morning. As always, his Remington rolling-block rifle was within easy reach.

* * * * *

As Donovan cautiously followed the trail approaching the mine, he stopped to ground tie Handsome Harry. Red spooked slightly when a covey of quail took flight off to the side of the trail, and he let out a small whine.

"It's all right, boy," Donovan assured the dog, rubbing his head. "Just some birds."

* * * * *

Ever alert to sounds, Emerson cocked his head and watched the birds fly over. He wasn't sure, but he thought he had heard a dog yip, not the kind of sound a coyote or wolf would make, but a dog. He dropped the half-skinned jack rabbit, grabbed up his rifle, and ran off into the forest, toward the high ground behind the mine.

* * * * *

The Mountie finally came to the end of the trail where the woods opened into a large clearing that had a cabin off to one side, and a mining shaft off to the other. Donovan's eyes scanned from left to right and back again, but the place looked deserted. There was no smoke coming out from the cabin's leaning chimney, no smell of wood burning. Lucas could see no sign of movement off by the mine entrance, either.

"Easy, Red. Not seeing anything doesn't necessarily mean that there isn't anything to see." He was talking to himself as much as to the dog, for, while he didn't see anything or anyone that would make him wary, he sensed a danger he hadn't felt in a long time.

"Let's take a look around, boy. Quiet," he cautioned as he thought he heard a scuffing sound. He waited, but all was silent again except for the ordinary sounds one hears in the great outdoors.

While Emerson was still climbing up to a better vantage point, Donovan searched the area carefully. The first thing he noticed was the number of footprints leading back and forth between the cabin and the entrance to the mine. As he bent down to get a closer look, he was thinking to himself: *Someone's been here … and not that long ago. Judging by the size of these boot prints, he's a big man.*

By now Red had picked up the scent of the rabbit and squirrel abandoned near the cabin door and trotted over to explore.

"All right, Red, we'll search the cabin first," he whispered. Lucas slung the Sharps rifle up under his arm into a ready position. As he approached the cabin door, he made sure to keep himself at an angle so he wouldn't be seen from the front window, even though he knew that if anyone were inside, his malamute would have warned him by now.

"What do you have there, boy?" he asked, watching as Red pawed at the dead animals. As he moved over, the half-skinned critter told him that not only had someone been here, but they had not left very long ago.

Donovan nudged the cabin's door with the barrel of his rifle, and, seeing no one inside its crude interior, he entered, taking notice of everything in the room.

"He's around here somewhere, Red, that's for sure," he said. "We'll find him, or my name isn't Donovan."

At the same time as Lucas was emerging from the cabin, Emerson made it to the top of the hill that overlooked the whole clearing. He quickly adjusted the telescopic sight on his Remington. When he caught sight of the intruder, Emerson was surprised to see a lone man walking around with a big dog. He moved, positioning himself behind a pile of rocks from which he could watch his stalker. As he started to bring up the rifle again, the clouds separated and for a moment the sunlight beamed right down the scope, temporarily blinding him.

Down below at the cabin, Donovan was assessing the situation, the Sharps still cradled in his arms. Red was tossing the rabbit pelt up and down and jumping around when Lucas suddenly caught a reflection of light up on the hillside that overhung the mine entrance.

Generally, the first rule of hunting—both of man and beast—is never to shoot unless you can clearly see what you are shooting at, but, in this case, Lucas didn't have to see, he knew instantly what it was. And he believed he and his brother had been bushwhacked before by this very same man. Besides, no one else had any business being here. Donovan knew that flash of light had been the reflection from the polished rifle barrel or the scope of Emerson's gun. Clear shot or not, Donovan would take no chances. He flipped the Sharps up and fired instinctively, aiming for the spot he could envision in his mind's eye. The Sharps was designed to take down a buffalo, and its bullet will destroy anything it hits.

Donovan's round smashed into the telescopic sight almost precisely at the same time Emerson was preparing to fire. Emerson was thrown back as the telescope literally exploded. Consequently, the bullet from his Remington was fired just a hair off of its intended target. It was enough to miss Lucas Donovan, but it was not entirely a miss.

In an instant Donovan was reloading and firing another round up at a cluster of rocks he believed sheltered Emerson. As he glanced down, he saw Red lying on his side, and panting.

Meanwhile, Emerson was recovering from the shock of the bullet's impact on his rifle. His face was bleeding from a dozen small cuts caused by the flying fragments of glass and metal.

Donovan dropped the Sharps, carefully scooping the dog up into his arms. Ignoring the danger, he ran as best he could, carrying the burden of his dog to his horse. Gasping for breath, he placed the big dog over the front of his saddle, and stood, breathing hard, before he mounted up.

Turning the horse and pulling back on the reins before he gave the black the spurs, he shouted as loudly as he could: "Jack Emerson, my name is Lucas Donovan, and I know you for the back-shooting, murdering bushwhacker that you are. I'll be on the street in the center of Bannack tomorrow at noon to face you … man to man! If you aren't there, everyone will know you for the sniveling coward you are. And if you don't show, I will come after you again and again until hell freezes over!"

With that he sent his horse into a lope down the trail, back toward town with all the speed his horse could muster.

* * * * *

Emerson heard the words echoing through the hills and was stunned. Not only had someone outshot him, but it had been accomplished by someone he'd never heard of, a name he didn't even recognize. Who in hell was this Lucas Donovan, anyway, and what the hell had put a burr under his saddle? The name Donovan held no significance to him whatsoever.

Emerson knew one thing was for sure. He would not refuse the man's challenge. He had called him a coward, and nobody could get away with calling any Emerson that.

Come noon, he would be there in the street to teach this fool a lesson.

CHAPTER TWENTY-THREE

Donovan galloped into town with the Red draped across his saddle. He practically slid the horse to a stop in front of the first man he came to in town.

"You got a veterinarian here?" he asked frantically.

The man took one look at the dog and nodded. "Sure do. His name's Robert Ellis."

"Quick, man, where do I find him? Is it far?"

"Nope, right down the street," the man replied, gesturing. "Go down there till it curves off to the left. Big two-story white house. Can't miss it. Doctor Bob lives upstairs and has his office on the first floor."

"Much obliged," Donovan said, spurring the exhausted horse onward.

When he arrived at the house, Donovan yelled as he pulled Red from the saddle, hoping someone inside would hear him. An attractive woman stood at the open door as Donovan came up the steps. He turned slightly to make his way through the door. He could feel the warmth of Red's blood on his hand.

"Is the doctor here?" he yelled, even though the woman was only two feet away. "Please?"

Just then, a tall thin man, perhaps in his early thirties, came out of the room to the left of the entry with some sort of book in his hands. He sported a full-but-closely-trimmed beard. He seemed to be absorbed in thought, but he as soon as he saw Donovan holding Red, he apologized and shifted away from the door, indicating to Donovan that the dog should be taken into the room from which he had just emerged.

"Here, bring your dog inside. I'm Doctor Ellis."

Shaking from the weight of the dog as well as fear of losing his longtime companion, Donovan hurried through the door.

"Put him on the table to the right, there … easy." Red whimpered weakly and twitched as the veterinarian proceeded to examine him. Ellis warned Donovan: "Please keep him steady." He listened to his heart. "What happened?" he asked Donovan, who the vet feared was going into shock.

Lucas poured forth what had happened without taking a breath, as if by talking he could keep Red alive. "The man who did this was gunning for me. My name is Lucas Donovan and I am a corporal with the Canadian North-West Mounted Police. I've been trailing that man all the way from Fort Macleod up in Alberta. I was close to cornering him outside of town, but Red passed in front of me just as he fired. Tried a bushwhack."

"A Mountie, huh? Well, Lucas, was it? … I need you to go and get my nurse. She's hanging out laundry in the backyard. Her name is Cheri. If we are going to save this big fellow, we need to get that bullet out. Now go."

Donovan bolted through the door and ran toward the back of the house. When he saw Cheri, he knew it was not the woman who had answered the door. He called out to her.

"I'm here. All right?" Cheri said calmly, as she hurried up onto the porch. "There's no need to yell. What do you need, sir?"

"I'm sorry for startling you, ma'am, but Doctor Ellis told me to come and get you. My dog's been shot … gotta get the bullet out … need your help."

Cheri gave Donovan's upper arm a light squeeze of assurance. Without saying anything else, she moved around him to get to Dr. Ellis. Donovan followed.

"Shave the hair away from the wound," the veterinarian said to Cheri as soon as she entered the room. "Start preparing the area. The straight razor's there."

Cheri was already clipping away the long hair with scissors before she began shaving. She looked up at the doctor and smiled. "I've got it, Doctor."

Red let out a whine which sent a shiver down Donovan's body. He leaned over the table to reassure the dog, stroking his head.

As Donovan stood there, he tried to distract himself by studying the room. It was large and clean. He noted that there were mirrors and gas lamps around which seemed to magnify the natural light coming through the front windows.

"Why do all the serious ones always have to have so much hair?" the vet asked impatiently, more to himself than anyone else.

While Cheri began to clean the area around the wound, the doctor mumbled to himself: "I'm going to make an ether cone to fit his head." He crossed the room, again mumbling to himself— "That'll work."—as he picked up a container about the size of a large coffee can. He proceeded to make a small hole in its side. Next, he took a glass funnel out from a drawer and shoved the tip of it into the hole he had made, and then packed the open end of the funnel with cotton strips. He came back to the table.

"You all right, Corporal? Now comes the hard work … getting the bullet out. I'm going to put your dog under … anesthetize him … using this ether. I can get into this fellow's abdomen by using it."

"Isn't that dangerous?" Lucas asked.

Dr. Ellis nodded. "It can be … and you need to understand that. But we have to get that bullet out, assess the damage … so we don't have much choice."

"I guess we don't," Donovan agreed, squeezing Red's chin. "You do much of this sort of thing? I mean in dogs, that is?"

The vet took a deep breath before answering. "Truthfully, there isn't much call around these parts for dog surgery. Folks don't spend their hard-earned money on dogs. What we veterinarians do out here in the West is horse, cattle, and swine … ranch and farm animals."

As the two were talking, Cheri had gathered up the instruments that would be needed for the surgery.

Dr. Ellis looked down at Red, ran his hand through his fur, and then addressed Donovan. "Well, I'll tell you, Lucas, I had a dog when I was a boy. Loved him dearly. I'm going to work on your dog, here, as if he were mine … that dog I loved."

Donovan nodded. "I get it, Doc. I will be eternally grateful … regardless of the outcome. And don't worry about getting paid, I can cover whatever it costs."

The veterinarian smiled at Cheri, commenting: "A client who can actually pay. How about that? I guess I'll have to raise my fee."

Cheri nodded her head. She had been working with Dr. Ellis for two years, mostly keeping things in order and assisting him as well as helping out his wife. Before coming to Bannack, she had worked with her father, who was also a veterinarian.

"Cheri and I are going to need your help, Lucas … a third set of hands," the vet explained to the corporal. "Think you are up to it? Can you handle some blood without passing out?"

"Sure, anything you need, Doc."

"Good. Now keep him still while I fit this over his head. He might fidget for a bit," the veterinarian said, before slipping the contraption he had fashioned over Red's snout. "Try not to breathe in those fumes, Lucas. Might want to pull your scarf up over your mouth and nose, like Cheri is doing." She had tied a white kerchief over her lower face before she began letting the ether drip from a small bottle down into the cotton that was stuffed inside the glass funnel.

Dr. Ellis began sprinkling a yellow liquid over the wound.

"What's that?" Donovan asked.

"Picric acid," the vet responded. "Some call it trinitrophenol, but the way I make it up it's called picrimol. It is an astringent that seems to disinfect the body tissues without doing too much damage to them. Seems to help cut down on postoperative infections. I've used it before."

Donovan barely nodded as he watched.

"Now, Corporal, that was your last question till I'm done. I want you to watch the ether drip. Cheri will guide you. She'll be watching Red's breathing pattern and his eye and ear reflexes. We don't want too much ether, nor too little."

The doctor slipped his spectacles on before he picked up a scalpel. Then he went to work over the big red malamute. "Making the initial incision," he said.

Occasionally Donovan glanced at the wall clock, which ticked loudly, making Donovan more aware of the passing of time.

Donovan didn't relax until he heard the vet say: "I can see the bullet. Get ready, Cheri."

Dr. Ellis addressed the Mountie some minutes later, without looking up from what he was doing. "Hard to tell how much blood he's lost, but I don't think it was that much. The bullet didn't nick any major organs that I can see, and there doesn't seem to be contamination. I've talked to doctors who have told me that when a bullet is fired, it heats up so much it can cauterize things. And that unless it hits a liver, kidney, or intestine, it doesn't seem to cause much infection. The danger is leaving the lead in there … it can poison the blood." He leaned in a little farther, saying: "Keep watching the ether … not too much."

Once the bullet had been removed, Lucas sensed that both the doctor and Cheri appeared to relax. The dog's open abdomen was inspected one last time, and towels were used to absorb the blood inside of the opening on the left side of his belly.

Once the doctor started suturing the wound, he smiled, which wasn't missed by Donovan.

"All right, Corporal, we can stop the drip now and remove that ether cone. Could you please take the cone to that basin over there? I should be finished suturing by the time our patient here awakens. But he'll be groggy for a while even then."

A huge wave of relief washed over Donovan, when Dr. Ellis said: "I'll keep him here for the night, keep him in a cage so he stays immobile, but I'm pretty sure he's going to pull through. As I said before, I don't get to work on dogs very often. But it was that dog of mine that made me want to go into veterinary medicine." Donovan had taken a seat in a chair near the desk. The doctor walked over, wiping his hands on a towel as he stationed himself at the desk chair.

"See that certificate on the wall? I didn't learn this stuff by merely apprenticing. No, sir! I studied day and night. Still do. We may be out in the sticks up here in Montana and on the edge of nowhere as far as Eastern city folks are concerned, but I am a graduate of the University of Iowa's College of Veterinary Medicine. There isn't any better school for this sort of study, except maybe that one you all have up there in Guelph," he added, with a smile.

"I've kept up on the latest procedures and techniques being used in the East on both human and animals. I apply these new methods and ideas whenever I can. I'm as good as it gets around here and I've had more practice with small animals than anyone else in the state. We've done everything we can for your dog."

* * * * *

Twenty minutes later, Donovan and the doctor were standing over the surgery table, their eyes burrowing into the eyes of Red. The big malamute was breathing more rapidly now and slowly his eyes were beginning to open.

Dr. Ellis patted Donovan's arm and then walked over to an oak cabinet. He took out several cotton sheets and began tearing them into long strips. "One more favor, please, Corporal. Lift him up by the hindquarters while I lift his front end." Then he addressed Cheri, instructing her to start wrapping Red's midsection with the strips of cotton.

She began the wrapping at the back of the dog, working steadily forward until just past the last ribs. Then she applied a sticky substance to the ends of the strips and patted the ends down. "Adhesive," she explained to the corporal. "Helps keep it bound."

"But isn't that a little too tight?" Donovan asked, concerned that the wrapping would interfere with his breathing.

"No," the veterinarian answered. "Doesn't go up that high. We need it tight though. I don't know exactly how it works, but we've known for some years now that after an operation like this, wrapping the area this way cuts down on the amount of internal bleeding. Also, there is a theory that the pressure from the bandage sends the blood forward to protect the heart. I don't know if it's true or not, but I don't believe it can do any harm."

The veterinarian bent over Red and lifted his lip slightly. "Nice pink color," he noted. He pressed down on the exposed gum with his right thumb and then released it quickly. "See how the gum gets white with my thumb's pressure, but when I release it the pink color quickly returns?"

The corporal nodded.

"Well, if a patient has lost too much blood or if his organs begin shutting down, it takes longer for color to return to the gum. Sometimes, it stays a pale gray or even white."

"And that's bad?"

Dr. Ellis nodded. "Very. There are studies about a syndrome they are calling shock. From what I gather from my studies, when the body is severely compromised, the blood goes deep trying to support the heart, the lungs, and the brain. That's why the skin gets a pale pallor and the body gets cold. You know, cold and clammy?"

"Sure, I've seen that," Donovan replied.

"It's because in this state of shock, there's no blood going toward the outside tissues of the body. It all pools inside. But that hasn't happened here with your dog. We seem to have gotten lucky so far. What's his name?"

"Red," Donovan answered.

"Red's gums are nice and pink and his breathing's regular." The doctor took a rag off a hook and washed his hands in the wash basin again.

"So we wait now?" Lucas asked.

"Well, what Cheri and I are going to do is keep him warm and comfortable," Dr. Ellis assured him. "As for you, Corporal, I suggest that you go back to the hotel, or wherever it is you are staying, clean up, and get some rest. There isn't anything else you can do right now. We just need to keep an eye on him. He should be kept quiet for a couple of days, should everything proceed as anticipated. If he makes it."

"*If* he makes it?" Donovan took a step toward the doctor, his boots making a loud noise on the floor. "I thought everything went well?"

Tossing the dirty wash rag and towel into a laundry basket in the corner, the doctor sighed. "It did, Corporal, as well as could have been expected, but Red isn't out of the woods quite yet. There's still the possibility of things like suture breakdown, wound swelling, pain, infection."

The concern on the Mountie's now pale face was obvious.

"Look, why don't you let me worry about Red, and you go get some dinner, some sleep. You can come back early in the morning. I'm up by five." Dr. Ellis paused before saying what he felt he had to ask: "And there's the man who did this, isn't there?"

Donovan nodded, his body tensing up at the mention of Emerson.

"Well, from what you've told me, it isn't going to be easy to catch him. You'll need to be one hundred percent to meet up with him, I would imagine. Now go. Red's in good hands."

Donovan bit his bottom lip as he nodded. "I'm sure of that, Doc. When Red wakes up, give him a pat on the head for me, will you? He doesn't like to be away from me."

"You can count on it," the vet said. "Just one thing more."

Thinking the vet might be referring to his fee, Donovan reached into his pocket for some of the gold sovereigns. "Oh, sure. I almost forgot. Just how much do I owe you, Doc?"

Dr. Ellis shook his head and put his hand on Lucas' shoulder. "I'm not referring to that. We'll settle up later ... when Red is ready to go home. What I meant was, after you catch this son of a bitch, let me know. I want to be there when they hang him." He shook his head and extended his hand. "Anyone who'd shoot a good dog like this deserves to swing."

Donovan took the vet's hand and thanked him.

"See you tomorrow, bright and early, Corporal," Dr. Ellis said, stifling a yawn. "Don't you worry about anything. I'll stay with Red. Never have left a critical patient alone and I won't start now."

Lucas smiled. "Thank you. Anything happens, send word to me at the hotel, would you please?"

"Certainly, Lucas," Dr. Ellis told Donovan.

CHAPTER TWENTY-FOUR

Donovan returned to his hotel room, destined to spend another restless night. To Lucas' way of thinking, he had once again been bested by this murderous renegade. First, he had lost his twin brother, and now there was a chance he might lose Red. All this loss because of one miserable outlaw named Jack Emerson.

Thinking about it, Lucas was almost physically sick. It wasn't fear that was twisting up his insides, however. You have to care about things in order to be afraid, but Donovan no longer cared about anything, except to avenge his brother's death and the shooting of Red. The anger that welled up inside felt like a someone was tearing out his insides.

The small pendulum clock on the wall slowly ticked the hours away, giving the Mountie too much time to think. While there was a possibility that Emerson might choose to run, Donovan somehow knew that wouldn't be the case. Come noon, they would face each other in the street for one final confrontation.

He had faced danger many times before in his line of work, but he had never faced it feeling so alone, with so many strikes against him. Still, overall, his had been a good life, and outside of the guilt he felt for never having repaid Jamie for saving his life twice, Lucas had no other regrets.

* * * * *

In the morning, Lucas was done wrestling his demons, and resolute in his determination to kill Jack Emerson. He sat up on the bed, missing Red's enthusiasm for the new day ahead, another adventure. He walked over to the small washstand that was against the wall and poured some water into the basin. He splashed his face and dried it, and then dressed.

The young Mountie then sat down at a small desk and took out a sheet of paper. At the top of the sheet he wrote: "Last Will and Testament of Corporal Lucas Donovan."

He inventoried his possessions and property. In spite of having seen more than his share of men lose their lives, never before had he even considered his own mortality. He had always felt too young to worry about such things, even since Jamie had been murdered.

He decided that if Red lived, he would bequeath him to the veterinarian, who had so candidly told him about his love for a childhood dog. Ellis seemed like a caring man and could certainly provide Red with a good home. If he were unwilling to take care of Red, well, then, he was certain he would find Red a proper home with a good family.

Any possessions of consequence back home in Canada, he would leave to the Mounties. He felt sure that the money from the sale of the ranch would be put to good use by the force. As for the money he had saved, he would leave that to Miss Victoria Marston. While she had not been in the forefront of his thoughts since their meeting, an unfamiliar feeling rose inside whenever an image of her unexpectedly popped into his mind. He felt it was a suitable gesture on his part for one who had made him feel so special.

He folded the paper, deciding he would ask for an envelope down at the front desk and then leave the document with the clerk. He got up and glanced over at the mirror above the wash basin. In the reflection he saw a man in plain clothes, just like any other man. *That's not who I am*, he thought. *If I go out … hell, I'm going out a Mountie.* From his bag, he pulled out his scarlet tunic and gray pants, the two pieces of his uniform he had brought along even though he had thought it was a bad idea at the time since he would not be in the service of the NWMP in the States.

Minutes later, Donovan stood facing the mirror in the most distinctive pieces of his dress uniform as a constable of the Canadian North-West Mounted Police. He buckled on his holster, checked the Webley. As an afterthought, he took out a folding pocket knife and used it to cut the flap from the Webley's holster. Donovan knew he could get a new regulation holster, and since he no longer had his Sharps rifle, he would have to depend solely on the revolver. At close range, speed with a pistol would make a huge difference and the flap would merely get in his way. Without the holster flap, his cross-draw would be significantly improved.

Donovan's intention all night long had been to shoot Jack Emerson on sight and damn the consequences. However, as he turned to study his profile in the mirror, the image before him seemed to say: *Right or wrong, good or bad, that is not how a Mountie behaves.* He thought of Jamie and knew that, if the tables were turned and he stood in Lucas' place, he would never just shoot a man, that the fight would have to be fair. He then thought of Victoria Marston and how difficult it would be, if he saw her again, to tell her that he had gunned Emerson down.

Donovan inhaled deeply. The words of the motto of the NWMP came to him: "*Maintiens le droit*," which means, "Uphold the right." He thought of the core values of the constables, values that Jamie personified—honesty, professionalism, integrity, respect, compassion, and personal accountability. He knew then that he had to face Emerson square on—and act according to the code of the force.

He looked around the room one last time, feeling the absence of his dog with whom he had such a strong bond. Donovan considered going to the vet's office first, but thought seeing Red would redirect his focus. Besides, he feared Red might get excited at the sight of him and he knew rest was most important for his recovery. Lucas decided he would go directly to the center of town and await his fate.

He closed the room door quietly and walked down the stairs. He left his will with the clerk after he had put it in an envelope. Once he was out on the street, Donovan put on his hat and pulled the brim down in front. He liked to wear the hat like that, pulled down low, keeping his face in shadow.

The morning was cool, but for a Canadian used to frigid air, he felt refreshed as a gust of wind hit him squarely. As he stood there on the plank walkway outside the hotel for a few minutes, Lucas reflected that life was good. He felt that it was as good a day to die as any other, if that was what was in the cards for him. He headed toward the center of town.

As he walked, he couldn't help noticing how people he passed were watching him closely, some were staring. In Canada, a Mountie's uniform was always impressive and demanded respect, but, here in the States, it apparently made for a rather unusual spectacle.

He was on the alert now, scanning the rooftops and the windows. He would not put it past Jack Emerson to try to shoot him again from hiding, as that appeared to be the usual way he worked.

Overall, the town was quiet, and the Mountie detected nothing out of the ordinary. A wagon went by and joined two others parked outside the feed store, while a couple of women entered the dry-goods store.

He took out his silver pocket watch and glanced at it. Eleven thirty. One half hour till noon and whatever it would bring. Lucas still had three blocks to walk until he reached the town center where he would wait for the man who had murdered his twin. Maybe killed his dog.

CHAPTER TWENTY-FIVE

Jack Emerson was furious. This stranger knew his name and had trespassed on his family's property while hunting him down. Not only that, but the man had insulted him, called him a coward. Worse yet, he had ruined the telescopic sight on his favorite rifle. The fact that Emerson had been in the process of trying to kill this man meant absolutely nothing to him. Even though his rifle was still perfectly functional, the scope was destroyed. And although he would not need it today, Emerson had liked the edge that scope gave him, and because it had been custom made to fit the Remington rolling-block, it was unlikely he would be able to replace it anytime soon.

After a quick breakfast of eggs and beans, together with a cup of bad coffee, Emerson mounted his bay horse and set out for the town of Bannack. He feared little as he rode, least of all any interference from the local law. Emerson had eliminated that threat weeks earlier when he had ambushed the local sheriff three miles outside of town, killing him with a shot between the eyes. Although it was unusual for him to do so, he had buried the lawman's body in a ditch and covered it with brush, which is why he knew no one would stand in his way today against the damned stranger.

Because Emerson had grown up in these parts, he knew exactly how long the ride to town would take. He had traveled this road hundreds of times through the years. He never carried a watch, so every once in a while, he would look up at the sun to gauge his progress.

Right as the sun was hitting its midway mark, Emerson reached the outskirts of Bannack. He carried the Remington rifle sideways across the saddle in front of him. He ran his hand over the rifle barrel where the missing scope should be mounted, reigniting his hatred of this man named Donovan. Carried lengthwise in his saddle's rifle sheath was the Sharps rifle he had found on the ground near his cabin. The one the stranger had dropped. Emerson had made up his mind this morning what he was going to do with it.

Normally he would have no compunction about assuring his own safety by ambushing an opponent, but, in this case, Emerson's curiosity got the better of him, which is why he was heading to the center of town for the showdown. Emerson wanted to see the face of the man who had insulted him and temporarily bested him, the one who had dared to challenge him, the one who had ruined his fine rifle scope.

Emerson stopped his horse a block short of the town's center and tied him to a hitching rail. He pulled the Sharps rifle from the sheath and headed to the spot where the two men were to meet.

The Sharps, like his Remington rolling-block, was also a single-shot firearm, but he had no ammunition for this particular Sharps since its caliber differed from his rifle. Emerson appreciated a fine gun as much as the next man, so if everything went as planned, he would keep it and buy bullets for it later.

Emerson walked down the middle of the east-side plank walk with a rifle in each hand. When he turned the corner and looked down the street, he stopped in his tracks for an instant when he saw the scarlet Norfolk jacket of the Canadian Mounties on a tall man, standing there, waiting for him.

Suddenly it made sense to the bushwhacker that the NWMP

would be after him, but what this particular Mountie was doing here in the States baffled him. Besides, Emerson knew they had no legal authority down here.

* * * * *

As soon as Corporal Lucas Donovan spotted Jamie's Sharps, he knew he was about to face the man he was after. He saw before him a bulky man with a neck the size of a bull. The description he had been given by Grant and Stanton had been accurate. Emerson was not particularly tall, perhaps five eight or nine, but what there was of him looked solid as a rock. He had scraggly hair and beard, and deep furrows were etched into his forehead.

The outlaw glared at his opponent as he approached confidently. Since the Mountie had his hat pulled down in front, Emerson couldn't make out his facial features, but what he could make out of the man meant nothing to him.

"You the one who was at my place yesterday?" he asked.

"I am," Donovan replied. "And I'm sure you know it."

Emerson laughed. "I know nothing of the kind, 'cept that you're gunning for me. Mind telling me why? After all, you Mounties got no authority down here."

It was Donovan's turn to laugh. "Truthfully, it doesn't matter a hoot in hell to me whether I have authority or not. This matter is personal. I shouldn't do this, but I'll tell you what … you give yourself up right now, come back with me to Canada, and I'll see that you get a fair trial. Otherwise, you won't leave here alive."

"Mighty big talker, ain't you?" the man-killer said boldly. "You Mounties have trailed me all over Canada without one bit o' success. Never even seen me."

"But I tracked you down now, didn't I?" Donovan said pointedly.

Emerson thought things over for a moment. "Wait a minute, you said it's personal. What do you mean by that?"

"You killed the wrong man, Emerson. Now it's time for you to pay."

"Pay? Why should I have to pay a law dog like you in a red clown suit?"

"Because of who you killed and how," Donovan replied.

"Well, it's my turn to make *you* an offer. Here, take this." He leaned down and skidded the empty Sharps rifle across the ground. It stopped several yards from the Mountie's feet. "My rifle against yours. Go ahead. Pick it up. It's loaded."

Donovan was certain that if he made even the smallest move toward the rifle, the outlaw would fire. Moreover, the Mountie sensed that Emerson was lying, that the Sharps would be empty. If, however, Lucas were to draw on the man, there was still a chance for success. Donovan was one of the best shots on the force, and he had calculated that he could cross-draw and fire his revolver before Emerson could get his rifle cocked and raised up to his shoulder to fire.

The Mountie slowly lifted his left hand and grasped the bottom of his pistol's holster in order to steady it. The movement was not lost on Emerson who moved his thumb up and over onto the Remington rifle's firing hammer. His finger was already on the trigger.

In a life and death situation, only a fool would give his opponent an edge, and Donovan was in no mood to make a noble gesture, such as stupidly letting this murderer make the first move.

Without another word, Donovan went for his pistol and was as fast as lighting. An open-holster draw from the waist can be blindingly fast, and at that range the Mountie knew he would not miss. What hadn't crossed his mind, however, was that Emerson might not have to raise and sight his rifle.

For a man as experienced as Emerson, it was almost reflex to cock his rifle and just flip its barrel slightly upward, shooting low, from the hip. Donovan took the rifle bullet straight in the stomach before he could get off a single shot.

The impact of the rifle bullet pitched Donovan backward and around. He was on the ground, face down. Upon impact, his hat had flown off, and the Webley slid out of his reach.

Satisfied, Emerson took a moment to reload his rifle. He grunted with pleasure and was about to turn and leave when he heard a groan coming from the man he had just shot dead.

He watched as Donovan lifted himself back up to his knees with great effort and then slowly turned back around to face his assailant.

As the man-killer turned, there was a look of pure amazement on Emerson's face. "Impossible. This rifle would take down a buffalo," he muttered to himself. Without thinking, he glanced down at the rifle's breech, wondering if somehow the cartridge had misfired.

The outlaw then looked up, and this time he raised the rifle up to his shoulder, intending to shoot the man right between the eyes. But, as he raised the gun and prepared to shoot, he hesitated, for this experienced man-killer always remembered the faces of those he had killed. Without his hat on, he could clearly see the Mountie's face.

Emerson lowered the rifle slightly. "You? I ... I killed you," he said, a shiver running down his spine. He was shocked to his core.

The pain in Donovan's belly was so profound it almost sapped him of his voice. "Apparently not," Lucas replied with a harsh cough.

"No, not just now. Back ... there. Out on that trail in Canada ... in the snow. I shot you right in the chest. I watched you die."

"Did you?" Donovan asked.

For perhaps the first time in as long as he could remember, Emerson was frightened. He had never confronted a ghost before. But ghost or no ghost, he had to bring an end to this man's life.

He tried to make his rifle move back to his shoulder, having convinced himself he was mistaken, that this man just looked like the man he had killed up there in the gully filled with snow. But again he stopped as he saw tears begin to trail down the cheeks of the Mountie. As he watched in disbelief, the man's chest began heaving as he sobbed heavily.

Emerson shook his head and laughed. "I never thought I'd see the day a Canadian North-West Mounted Policeman would be on his knees crying like a baby. Afraid, are you, tough guy?"

Lucas shook his head, ran the sleeve of his shirt across his face. "They're not for me," he said.

"No? Then who they for?"

"They're for him," Donovan said, nodding his head in Emerson's direction.

"Who?" Emerson said. "I think you've ..." He stopped talking as he heard the growl behind him. "What the ...?" He swung around in time to see an enormous red-and-white dog leaping at him, wearing some sort of swaddling. Emerson tried to back up, but he was too slow. The dog landed on him, knocking him over, sending the Remington flying. Emerson had not had enough time to react.

Red attacked him with the fury of a starved wolf, biting deep into his shoulder, shaking his head, ripping fabric and tearing flesh. Emerson screamed in both pain and fright.

The pain was excruciating, but Emerson's wits were coming back into focus—at the same time, the dog was weakening as he tried to fight on. After a few moments of thrashing back and forth, which had turned him around, Emerson was able to fling the dog from his arm and away. The dog yelped when he hit the ground. Emerson got up and reached for the Remington rifle with the arm that hadn't been torn into by the dog. He pulled it over and tried with one hand to raise it and point it in Red's direction.

"This one's for Jamie," he heard a voice say from behind. Quickly he turned back around just in time to see the Mountie, still on his knees, but with a large revolver in his hand. The Webley's heavy bullet penetrated his head right between his eyes. Darkness came instantly, as Emerson fell over backward.

The big malamute struggled to its legs and hobbled slowly over to the man who had raised him from a pup. Lucas hugged the big dog, tears still streaming down his face as he thought of Jamie. Red was whimpering again, but this time it was not from pain. It was because of the joy he felt at this reunion with his master.

Dr. Ellis came running up to where Donovan and the dog had fallen.

"I've been chasing him," the vet said, slightly out of breath. "That big brute of a dog managed to get out of his cage and sneak out the door at some point. Only one day after surgery! I never saw anything like it. He really doesn't like being away from you, does he?"

"Will he be all right?" Lucas asked, as he tried to determine if Red's wound was bleeding again.

The veterinarian stooped down and did a quick check of the dog. "Aside from a few new scratches, I don't think there is any great damage done." He shifted the remnants of the bandage, most of which had unwound and lay strewn on the ground, to examine the bullet wound. "The sutures seem intact. His pulse and his color are good. Yeah, I think with rest and care, he'll be all right."

"Thank God," Lucas sighed, pushing himself up to his feet with some help from Dr. Ellis.

"Whoa, wait a minute man. I saw that you were shot." The vet pointed at Lucas' belly. "Right there. How the hell are you still alive?"

Donovan pulled open the tunic and shirt to reveal his money belt. "I guess money belts are good for more than just hiding coins."

"Well, I'll be damned!" Dr. Ellis exclaimed. "The coins must've stopped the bullet."

Both men laughed and spontaneously hugged each other.

"Now let's get this dog of yours back to my office. I need to get a new bandage on him, and you look like you could do with something for the pain."

Donovan holstered the Webley, and then stooped down to

recover his hat. Bending over, hurt more than he had anticipated. "Yeah, I guess so, Doc," he groaned, as he straightened up. "Got anything for pain, about ninety proof, made in Canada?"

"Coming right up," the vet said, leading the pair slowly back toward the two-story house.

CHAPTER TWENTY-SIX

Two weeks later, Dr. Ellis and Corporal Lucas Donovan were sitting at the dinner table in the vet's dining room. Lying under the table, close to his master's feet, was a large red-and-white malamute. The bandages were off, and Red was now declared fit for duty.

As Lucas glanced down at his dog, Dr. Ellis observed: "Remarkable healing powers, that one. Wasn't sure, at first, he'd make it."

"Quitting just ain't in him, Doc," Lucas replied. "No back up or give."

"I might say the same about his owner. But I noticed you keep checking Red's fur. I promise, it will soon grow back. A couple of months from now, and you'll never notice a thing. Dogs don't seem to scar as easily as humans do."

"Sure hope you're right," Lucas replied.

"Have I been wrong about anything so far?" Ellis asked.

Lucas chuckled. "No, not yet. And you were right about this dinner, too. Best chicken dinner I've had in … I can't remember how long."

"Yeah, my wife's a great cook." The doctor patted his stomach. "A couple more years of this and I expect I will have the big round belly of Saint Nicholas."

The veterinarian's wife entered the room. "I heard that, Robert. You do, and I'll run off with a slender man." She laughed and looked fondly over at Lucas. The three had become good friends over the past weeks. "Maybe I can find a nice young Mountie."

Lucas choked on the water he was trying to swallow, followed by an uncomfortable blush.

Robert Ellis laughed and reached over and patted his friend on the back. "Careful there."

The vet turned to his wife. "Besides, Lucy, from what Lucas has been telling me, I suspect he's already spoken for."

"Really? And who might the lucky girl be?" she asked. "Tell me about her?"

Lucas cleared his throat and hesitated. He was obviously embarrassed. "Well, I'm not so sure you'd describe it as truly being spoken for. We met only briefly, so I can't tell you that much about her. But I did get the feeling she was interested ..." He let his words trail away.

"And are *you* ... interested, Corporal Donovan?" Lucy asked. She looked over at her husband and winked.

Lucas thought a moment and replied with a smile. "Yes, ma'am, I surely am."

"This girl got a name?" she asked.

"Yes, ma'am. It's Vicki. Victoria Marston."

"So, is she attractive?" Lucy asked.

"She must be quite a looker. Our young constable here has done nothing but mumble to himself about her for the last week," Dr. Ellis replied.

"Looks aren't everything, Robert," Lucy remarked sharply.

"Why do you think I married you? Besides the cooking that is," Robert teased her playfully.

"Well, I never!" Lucy exclaimed, feigning outrage as she stood up. "Will you never grow up and stop behaving like such a clod? And in front of guests." She turned toward the kitchen in a huff, but just before leaving the dining room, she paused at the door, and looked back lovingly at her husband. "I'm getting the pie. It's for Lucas here. At least he behaves like a gentleman."

"That's just because he's Canadian. They're all like that," her husband joked.

"Well, maybe you should spend some time up there yourself."

"I would, but then who'd be here to listen to all your criticisms?"

"Well, I never," Lucy said, and left the room.

"You two seem very much in love," Lucas observed, once Lucy disappeared in the kitchen.

"Yep, five years and still as great as at the beginning."

"Must be nice," Lucas said, smiling.

"Yes, it is. Marriage is kinda like being tickled."

"How so?" the Mountie asked.

"Well, you still feel like laughing, even when it begins to hurt."

"I heard that!" Lucy yelled out from the kitchen. "No pie for you!"

Both men laughed. "She doesn't really mean it. I suspect she's trying to fatten me up, so I won't be attractive to the ladies anymore," Ellis said loud enough for his wife to overhear.

Lucy entered the dining room with a tray of plates and the pie. "I don't have to," she said, continuing the banter. "You weren't all that attractive to begin with."

"Won you over, didn't I?" the vet said, and winked.

"He does have a point there," Lucas said.

"He just tired me out. I got tired of fighting him off, and finally just surrendered," Lucy explained.

"Right," her husband replied. "I chased her until she finally caught me." He punched Lucas softly in the arm as if pleased with his own joke.

"So, changing the subject back to where it belongs, just where is this lovely lady now?" Lucy asked.

"She's in Helena. Or so I understand. We only met the one time, on the train on the trip down from Alberta," Lucas explained.

Lucy Ellis put down the pie and looked at her guest with her hands firmly on her hips as if sizing him up. "An attractive single young girl, who you are crazy about, is alone in Helena, Montana, and you're still here? What kind of men are they letting into the Mounties these days, anyway?"

"Well ...," Lucas stammered.

"She's right about that and you know it," Robert Ellis said, nodding in agreement.

"Well, it's not like I haven't had things to do. And then of, course, there's Red."

At the sound of his name the big dog barked.

"No problem there anymore, as far as I can see," the veterinarian said.

"Lucas, you know we love you to death and should you ever decide to abandon policing that horrid Canadian wilderness, you will always be welcome here. But for now, I think you should get your arse out of that chair and go look for her."

"Arse? Really, Lucy?" Robert laughed.

"I am a western woman, and I will speak as I see fit ... when the occasion calls for it," Lucy replied stridently. She turned back to Lucas. "So, Corporal Donovan, constable of the Canadian North-West Mounted Police, what are you waiting for?"

Her husband chipped in. "Yeah, I thought you Mounties always got their woman. So, what are you waiting for?" the vet added.

"Nothing I guess." Lucas looked back and forth between the two of them and shrugged. "It appears I will be heading out first thing tomorrow."

"But not before you finish the pie I baked," Lucy ordered, slapping aside her husband's finger as it inched toward the pie crust. "You'll be lucky if I let you have the crumbs after how you've behaved tonight." It took a moment, but then they all broke out laughing.

CHAPTER TWENTY-SEVEN

The journey to Helena felt long to Donovan as he worried how Victoria Marston would react when she saw him. The first day of the trip, Lucas had taken it slow so as not to overexert his dog, but Red quickly regained his former strength and once again seemed happy to run alongside his new friend, Handsome Harry.

After arriving in Helena, he stabled his horses. Then he checked into the hotel, got a good night's sleep, and visited the local barber. By the end of the second day, he knew where Victoria Marston lived.

Arriving at the doorstep of a large old two-story home early in the evening, Lucas dusted off his scarlet jacket.

"Well, boy, here goes nothing," he said to Red, who sat down at Donovan's feet. The Mountie hesitantly used the door knocker to announce his presence.

Unsure of the reaction he would get from the lady after so long an absence, Lucas fidgeted nervously while he waited for someone to answer his knock. Donovan would be the first to admit he feared no man. He was never timid or unsure of what course of action to take while pursuing a suspect, but pursuing a beautiful woman was new and unknown territory to him. Although the Mountie was filled with anticipation, there was always that uncertain feeling in the back of his mind that it had all been an illusion, or that she had somehow changed her mind. After all, they had only known each other a short time.

After what seemed an eternity, he heard footsteps approaching on the other side of the door. He cleared his throat and wiped his brow just before the knob turned and the door opened.

"Ahem. Ah, hello, Miss Marston. I don't know if you remember me, but—"

"Lucas!" Vicki exclaimed as she flung herself at him and planted a kiss on his lips.

"I guess that answers that question," Lucas said, smiling.

She bent down and gave Red a big hug, and the dog wagged his tail as happily as ever. When she finally ushered them both into her home, he had one more question to ask.

"So, I was wondering, Vicki, how would you feel about living in Canada?"

THE END

ABOUT THE AUTHOR

R. W. Stone inherited his love for western adventure from his father, a former Army Air Corps armaments officer and horse enthusiast. He taught his son both to ride and shoot at a very early age. Many of those who grew up in the late 1950s and early 1960s remember it as a time before urban sprawl, when Westerns dominated both television and the cinema, and Stone began writing later in life in an attempt to recapture some of that past spirit he had enjoyed as a youth. In 1974 Stone graduated from the University of Illinois with honors in Animal Science. After living in Mexico for five years, he later graduated from the National Autonomous University's College of Veterinary Medicine and moved to Florida. Over the years he has served as President of the South Florida Veterinary Medical Association, the Lake County Veterinary Medical Association, and as executive secretary for three national veterinary organizations. Dr. Stone is currently the Chief of Staff of the Veterinary Trauma Center of Groveland, an advanced level care facility. In addition to lecturing internationally, he is the author of over seventy scientific articles and a number of Westerns, including *Trail Hand* (2006), *Badman's Pass* (2016), and *Across the Río Bravo* (2017). Still a firearms collector, horse enthusiast, and now a black belt–ranked martial artist, R. W. Stone presently lives in Central Florida with his wife, two daughters, one horse, and three dogs.